Released on 5th November 2023

Written & created by: Jack Cliffe

Cover art: Jack Cliffe

Additional thanks: Andrew, Dayle, Dylan, Ryan O, Sean, Sue, Zayn, And my family

This book is the first in the Advance Heroes series. It is recommended you start here so you can follow the storyline properly.

Contents:

Advance Heroes

Volume 1

The Scarlet Blade

Chapter 1

A New Story Unfolds

Betwixt the pages of a book lies the nose and eyes of a young magic teacher, Kevin. Reading a relatively old fictional novel in the middle of a mock exam, somewhat based on "true" events of an ancient war, almost lost completely to time.

— The year was 1486. There was once a family of three royal siblings who each ruled a kingdom in a faraway land. —

— Be that as it may, at a time- this world coexisted with our own. Through the once mystic gateways that are built around the globe, awaited you three vastly divergent civilizations, unique in all their own ways and governed by their respective royal leaders: —

— A king of blue, cool as sub-zero. A king of purple, beautiful and benevolent. And a traitor queen of red. —

— Raised upon their independent ideals, they took the triplet thrones of their world after their parent's sorrowful death, and the three got along as well as brothers and sisters should, until one vexed day... the red, bloody queen betrayed her brothers who loved her so; she left her kingdom to wilt and die. The king of blue still wracked with grief from the loss of his parents could not bear the distress and threatened to seize both siblings' lives if they ever stood against his reign. —

— The blood red queen hadn't seen her family for months and years on end. She created freaks of nature to observe

her home world as she hid under the asylum of another realm, away from her brothers who wept for her return so. —

— She roared with the power of thunder to her new people who she stole under her wing their freedom. "My brothers have waged war on me and this kingdom, if you wish to save your own lives then you will fight for me alone, hear the sound of our blades against their own!" War echoed through the poor kingdom's ears, they were wracked with shock and horror at her declaration of war- their freedom in the palm of her wicked hand, yet they refute her declaration with the rage of sun above. Yet the malevolent monarch held fast her wicked decree and threatened to slay all those who betray her, and stain them redder than her own crimson locks. —

As he pulls himself from the deep immersion of the book gripped firmly in his hands, the class teacher Kevin, looks up from his desk and gazes toward his class to behold half of them with heads on their desks, napping the period away or playing around with flickering magic the ichor of goldenrod and honey.

Closing his book with a careful hand so as not to damage its near fading hard cover, he steps up from the seat he was so comfortably parked in, followed by a short but sharp screech against the stone floor. With a flick of his index finger, all manner of magic present in the room is swallowed into his open palm. A spectacle to behold, spiralling in a flaming whirl of auburn and amber. Kevin's emerald-green eyes gaze into the flames that flutter and dance around his hand before dispelling it with a loud but harmless ***bang*** to wake up the pupils sleeping on their desks with a heart-jolting shock.

“You all know the rules about pratting around with magic in the classroom. Just because the rooms fireproof doesn't mean you can tempt fate.” He scolds sternly. “If some of you plan on going up in smoke before you graduate then I can always make tomorrow's practical lesson another written test about fire safety instead?”

Scanning around the room for guilty faces, he slams his hands on the cold desk and then finishes the lesson by calling out to his unenthusiastic pupils with an equally uninspired, long-winded breath. “It's half three, your dismissed- I'll see you all tomorrow.”

Chairs and desks once more screech against the hard stone floor with a glass-shattering wavelength. *What a noise...* He thought to himself. As the teenagers gather their bags and coats without a moment's hesitation, they pour out of the room in a cluttered fashion in a race to see who can get home first. The last of them leaves the stone void and closes the heavy heatproof-glass door with a loud echoing wave, bouncing around the room and through Kevin's ears.

Day after day classes never change for him, there's always a pupil who just can't pay attention or one that plays around with magic during a lecture, or a pupil that needs to be told of multiple times per lesson. Kevin knows in his heart that they're a clever lot; they just lack enthusiasm- much to his dismay he worries that perhaps his carefree mentality rubs off on them too much.

A shroud of silence then wraps the room in its comforting cloak to only be torn off with another echoing sound as Kevin slides into his chair and plants his face onto the hard, cold desk; letting out a long, exaggerated sigh... He groans and mumbles as he shimmies around in agitation praying tomorrow's day will be any different, though as a teacher he knows that may just be wishful thinking.

The loud, scraping door stumbles once more as Kevin looks up. He basks upon a familiar figure, clad in pale pear green with an over-filled bag of magic equipment, spell books and a friendly wisp like conjured companion perched on the sagging middle of the satchel. He's an old friend of Kevin's- Samuel Ortiz, though students and teachers alike call him Thome. Nobody really knows where the nickname came from, but Kevin's opinion is that it simply comes from the word tome, with a tad more flourish. Though according to student gossip, the real reason they all call him Thome is that he gets upset when people mispronounce or misspell his surname. 'Ortiz.'

Joining Kevin with his hypocritical head-on-the-desk session, Thome whisks up a chair with a spur of focused force magic, grinding and rumbling across the floor- His singular long black braid curls over his shoulder. He speaks with his usual entitled tone as his little glowing friend, Ethos zips around and plops down on the stone table.

"You look down, Kevin. Have you had another boring day? It's only as exciting as you make it, you know." He says, patronising him like a child.

Kevin replies with a snarky grin. "Oh nooo~, today was great! What gave you that funny idea??" He sighs. "Sitting in here all day with the same four grey walls, let me tell you; gets super boring, super-fast, no matter how much excitement your force into the day. At least I get to go outside tomorrow now that Christine has signed the health and safety forms. Now I can teach the kids with zero attention span some spellcasting. Whoopee..."

Though he would be lying if he said he was devoid of *all* excitement, even though tension fills his spaced-out mind like water in a flooding room.

The two share a moment of silence, something Kevin's been craving all day before getting up; notes spilling from Thome's bag. Kevin quickly rises and reaches to pick up the triple dozen scraps of paper his friend dropped, though Thome makes a swing of his foot and lifts two fingers into the air, he whips up a controlled yet powerful gust of wind that circles the room creating a pleasant draft. closing his spell, he binds his pages with a simple ring of light; tucking them away inside his already stuffed bag. Kevin gets up and grabs his things and the two depart, making their way to the staff room in the fire magic district.

The Carvina College of Arcane where the two work has had a district for wind, earth, aqua, nature and force magic for decades, though the flame department had only just been erected around seven years before Kevin got the job there. The college is smaller than most academic facilities that focus on magic training and it's far from the grandest, especially when you look at the flame district. Fire magic to nobody's surprise is highly dangerous, even if controlled by the most skilled mage. According to the Grand Mistress all rooms in the flame magic district are made purely of non-flammable materials, and still somehow somebody manages to set the building on fire at least once a year.

The fire magic building isn't even connected to the main building and rests quietly in the corner of the grounds, shadowed by the main college. The staff room here is also unfortunately grey, chilly and drab.

“This place is a mess...” Thome grumbles to himself, sweeping his finger along the wall, painting his fingertips grey with the ashen state of the brickwork.

“You have five other staff rooms to choose from, so take your pick.” Kevin sighs in response. “You're able to roam around the whole college campus just because your Hyper-Real power lets you use all the elements instead of just one or two like a normal person.”

Thome scratches the back of his head, slightly pulling apart a braid in the process; he replied with dynamism. “Well, at least you can get to point A to B at Mach speeds. the rest of us are forced to **walk** through the college. If anything, you're the lucky one out of all of us, Kevin. Though your super-speed doesn't make you the best mage here- I very well intend to surpass you and win the power and be the greatest mage in the country!”

“Yeah, I know, you never shut up about it...” Kevin mumbles through his fatigue.

After walking for a while at a leisurely pace Kevin and Thome reach the room where the staff of the very few flames classes commune when on break. There are large shelves made of marble with smooth purple granite trimmed around the edges, and the room smells of soot and the weak underpowered vanilla incense oils they try and use to damp out the smell.

The shelves are gorged with volumes upon volumes of artefacts and useless junk. Wherever you turn your head you're greeted by a burning flame on the wall held in the embrace of a dull looking sconce with a seal around it; there's always fire around. The pair sit in here for a while when all the students go home, it's not much of a place to sit but it's better than nothing they suppose.

Thome sits, collected with his bag to his side and Ethos on his lap, scratching her head with his finger whilst they talk. “This place needs a new lick of paint...” He spits.

“Like I said- If you don't like it you go to one of the other staffrooms. Not like they can kick you out with your fancy multiment.” Kevin snaps back.

After six hours of sitting and teaching, Kevin kicks his legs up for another few minutes of even more sitting, only difference this time being that he has company and a hot cup of tea. Thome bumps Kevin's broad shoulders, splashing a few boiling droplets of tea onto the floor below- he then averts his gaze towards a big lady with an imposing aura across the room- the Grand Mistress; she gives Kevin and Thome a lot of high praise. Though Thome thrives on praise and worship, Kevin doesn't see where it all comes from. It may be true that his magic is beyond others' abilities, but he scorns boasting; he likes to keep to himself, away from peeping ears and spying eyes.

Although Christine had her back turned against the two, she managed to sense the two boys were near, either that or she just saw them walk in, even though not a single sound came from their entry. Christine sat up and trotted towards them, clipping and clopping her heels on the ground like a horse- the aura around Thome grew thicker and tenser- …and Kevin just doesn't care.

She's a delight to be around in actuality. She's very boisterous but funny at the same time, the kind of woman who gives off a strong quality, a proud and thick-skinned vocal powerhouse who commands respect in a gentle but authoritative way. And despite comments on her stature, she stands firm and laughs in the face of insults, solid as a mountain though... That loud and boisterous part is exceptionally true.

“Hello, Kevin dear~ Just the man I wanted to see!” She chimes while rolling her curled brown hair between her fingers. “How are you both doing today? Are you ready for your practical lesson tomorrow, Kevin dear?”

He nods with uneasy duplicity and replies- no brand of eye contact. “Yeah, I'm really looking forward to it. Cheers for signing the safety forms and all that other technical.”

Christine bends down further and looks Kevin dead in the eye; a cold rumbling shiver darts down his spine as the eye of Medusa turns his soul to stone; her gaze alone being enough to see right through him.

“You don't look like you're being very honest young man, and you don't sound it either- you get all coy and conventional when you feel cooped, I know!” She sings. “Listen dear, this is your first practical lesson in four- no, five years! You've made mistakes, but you've learned from them and I'm positive it won't burden you again~ I've even been courteous enough to rearrange Thome's Friday timetable, just so he can be your assistant teacher for that period!”

Thome shoots up at blinding speeds as if he'd sat on a whole box of pins. He stutters with sudden, pent anxiety in his voice. “W-with all due respect ma'am! I can't possibly help tomorrow; I have exams to mark- I don't want to be a burden to Kevin by getting in the way and-”

Christine bends up from starring Kevin in the face relieving him of the ice-cold tension. She waddles over to Thome who twitches nervously. He jolts back as she leans in closer, pushing the walls of his personal bubble. “No ifs or buts from you either Sammy~ you two are working together tomorrow and that's final. You'll be a great help to Kevin in case anything goes wrong- G.M.'s orders!" She yodels with glee.

With nothing left to retaliate with, the once again defeated Thome breathes an audible sigh, "Yes Ma'am..."

With a big smile on her face, she waves goodbye and swings around; she walks back to the sunken couch she was sitting on, only to quickly shoot her eyes towards the old CRT television in the dusty corner of the room. It's yet another fire magic teacher's problem, cheap TVs mean less cost if it gets turned into a blob of hot, molten plastic. The news had caught everyone's attention.

Two female reporters on the flickering screen spoke with a crackling voice introducing a man with pale white hair and pointed ears along with a taller, more burly looking man of navy-blue locks.

The man smiles as the camera transitions to the man of pale hair. He speaks with a silver tone. "The last remaining World Gates have been reconstructed across central England and northern Blanc. Mercural kind is reconnecting with human society after approximately five hundred years apart! In addition, the world of Silvalon now officially welcomes all humankind back into our own society and welcomes people of all backgrounds with open arms!"

The reporters pull up their papers and talk over some pre-recorded footage; their joint demeanour more serious and sterner. "In other news, similar portals have been seen pre-planted around the areas listed on the screen now. Reports show that these portals without any kind of frame or main structure supporting them are conjure summoning portals, which have been somehow releasing unmanned conjures who are roaming the streets and causing chaos all over the Darchester, Lalstrun, Mordale and Carvina areas. Please stay well clear of any suspicious conjures and report it to your local arcane office as soon as physically possible. Thankyou." The reporter then repeats the local warning in a perfectly identical way as if she herself was pre-recorded.

After that, they changed the topic quickly and began talking about less important things like cats stuck in trees and such. Things that Kevin can't necessarily hear because the rest of the fire magic teachers are in uproar over the news report.

Thome gets up and levitates their finished mugs to the sink with the use of some cleverly used lumen magic; drawing a hand from his own shadow and stretching it to the sink with relative ease.

"Didn't you want to go home?" he asks quietly, readjusting his bag strap that's always falling from his small shoulders.

"Yeah, why not. Beats being deafened by this lot." Kevin replies.

The two of them trot along out the door after waving goodbye to the grand mistress and into the grand open yard. The streetlamps have just turned on, beaming down onto the evening pavement that slowly creeps with the cold of the coming night. Lamps with round glass globes hang above their tiring heads as they make their way outdoors. Kevin reflects on the smell of the countryside that awaits him on his travels back home.

Carvina is a long walk away from where he lives in Lalstrun, though getting from one place to another is a literal breeze for him. He bids Thome farewell and stretches his legs, preparing himself a spot on the street. He presses his heel down at destructive speed before kicking off the footpath at 200mph, leaving only a tail of wind, embers and dust behind.

Mach speeds are an obviously dangerous thing to handle, and most would easily slam into a wall and break their entire skeleton. He's hugged many walls many-a times before though and yet his bones have been completely fine- though the expression that strikes his face every time this happens shows it still hurts like murder...

Blasting past and leaping over obstacles; his reflexes sharper than a panther, Kevin soars through the roads and glides through the fields. The naked eye would trade ten million colour sight to be able to see him bolt through the countryside at these unfathomable speeds. Sprinting through Carvina and its neighbouring town Darchester in minutes flat, he makes a sudden scraping halt as his momentum scars the path beneath his feet.

At last, he arrives at his house in the countryside, a small, two-bedroom cottage on a flat hill in Lalstrun where his sister Leah and himself live. His noisy halt shook the old wooden sign that reads his surname 'Marrowald' and the racket it caused alerted Leah that he was finally home.

She opens the deep blue door, mounted with stained glass in the pattern of a colourful bird. She's always happy to see him return home after work as all families should be. She has dinner prepared by three forty-five. Behind her stands Kevin's favourite feline conjure and best friend - Mobbee. Standing on his back legs like a cat from a cartoon, he waves his front paws and makes inaudible, but very pleased noises at Kevin's return as he hobbles down the path and into Kevin's arms. The wind catches up behind him from his run and blows the door wide open.

He looks at his dear sister with an amused face, holding back giggles and laughter at her windswept hair. "I uh... *may* have gone a bit overboard with my run today, ha-ha."

Kevin walks in, lifting his cute bundle of fur over his shoulder as Leah shuts the blue, oak door behind them. Mobbee starts to play with Kevin's windswept hair with his paws, taking it between his claws and purring happily.

He's a very old friend of Kevin's, ever since he was a boy Mobbee has been by his side and helped him through every hardship along the way. As far as conjures go he can't do anything too special like fly or breath fire- but his very presence feels soothing to the soul. And for Kevin, he wouldn't have it any other way.

He plops his furry friend down and perches himself on the couch with a pillow behind his back. Mobbee waddles in and out of the kitchen with a glass of fresh-squeezed orange juice and places it carefully on the table.

"Juicy for dada!" He babbles with his gargly feline voice.

"Thanks, Buddy!" Kevin replies. Mobbee crouches down, aiming for the absent spot on the couch; a quick pounce follows. He performs an always accurate landing and crawls over to Kevin's tired lap on all fours and curls around him like a long, fuzzy pillow.

Leah walks in with her grandma's old tea tray. On it lies two piping hot cups of tea. One light and one dark- typical for Kevin to have a milky brew. Now it strikes him that he has two drinks waiting for him on the rattan tea table... Orange juice and tea. "Which to choose...?" He ponders out loud.

Leah heckles at his contemplation. "I think you should start with your tea before it goes cold. You can always take that orange up with you to bed, yeah?" Though he misses Leah's suggestion and continues to ponder. What a simple thing for him to turn into a triviality- his constantly absent mind confuses itself over two equally tasty drinks.

He finally decides to take his sister's advice, picking up the boiling hot mug, he takes a sip from the wide mug regretting it almost instantly as his tongue is scolded by the hot tea. His eyes squint, trying not to make a scene, he swallows the burning liquid as it scolds his throat.

Without thinking he starts to drink the juice at hyper-fast speeds to cool his mouth down, gasping for air between gulps. Before he knew it the entire cup of juice was gone, leaving none for later.

Leah speaks while trying not to giggle at Kevin's misfortune. "That'll teach you to wait until your brew has cooled down, won't it? Anyway, how's work? I remember you told me you'd get to do some field lessons again. How are you feeling about it?" She asks curiously.

He stares into the glass he now holds empty as he digs deep into his mind. *Well... How am I feeling about it?* The words echo and bounce around in his mind like a clown stuck in a bouncy castle without an exit. As he finds the words to make his reply, he rests the glass down on the coffee table shakily, not having a spare hand to steady ether.

He murmurs. "Well, to be frank with you I feel excited, but I'm worried I'll make the same mistake again... I almost got fired that time for severe arcane damages- which wasn't even my fault to begin with. The college should have built their walls properly and then nothing would have been destroyed in the first place."

He continues to ramble; his face begins to appear more stressed and far less mellow than usual. Kevin's whole body begins to tense and tighten before Mobbee carefully gets up from his twitching lap and begins to pat his face with his soft, small, gentle paws. He gargles out a loving purr and helps Kevin calm down. His breathing slows and Leah gets up and wraps her arms around her shivering kin.

“Sorry, I shouldn't have brought that up. I know you still hurt about what happened. How about we do something else?”

He then takes a few deep breaths, relishing the fact that his sister and loyal cat are willing to listen to his troubles. The siblings sit for a while after Kevin had calmed down somewhat quickly, Leah sits back in her armchair with a creak and a squeak. They banter and talk about the latest gossip together while flicking through the TV channels. Kevin pets Mobbee's fluffy, grey fur whilst Leah aggressively jabs the squishy buttons of the unresponsive remote.

“It won't work any better the harder you press the buttons, Loo.” He speaks.

“It knows fear.” She responds humorously.

the news flicks onto the TV once more- this time, at a much better quality. The generic-looking intro flies on screen as a cacophony of colours spirals around an image of the globe, before zooming into the UK like every news intro does; a fade-out swallows the screen to then choke up the news presenters waiting at their desks.

Leah scoffs “Bah. Reruns, wanna watch something else? It's always depressing stuff anyway.”

Kevin replies with haste. “Nah leave it on, I saw this today, but I might have missed an important smidge.”

Leah and Kevin mindlessly gawk at the TV in the corner as the news begins. The generic soundtrack fades into the background as the same well-kept women as before appears on screen and begin talking about the news. Kevin pays sharp attention to the news as Leah lounges around on her chair, slowly kicking her legs up and down as she opens a magazine, fully distracted.

The ladies on the TV speak the same things as last time; nothing new here. The two presenters swap over to the weather forecaster who speaks in a posh voice. “Tomorrows weather will be bright and sunny with little chance of rain and clouds!”

“At least it's gonna be sunny tomorrow. That's peace of mind, I guess.” Kevin reassures himself.

“It's always the opposite of what they tell you anyway.” Scoffed Leah, reading the latest magazine in magic supplies. She doesn't watch the news often because of all the politics and repetitive stories they talk about. She prefers to read something and have the news in the background- just in case they say something *worthy* of listening to.

She's currently reading a magazine on magic supplies because she creates custom magic-encrusted jewellery. Her hobby and job stem from her gran who always used to make enchanted jewellery to sell on the markets. Though this is only a secondary income source for her as her main occupation takes the name of arcane healer as she wields the element of aqua, which makes her a potent emergency doctor. She works with small wounds and common ailments such as cuts, bruises and colds that would take weeks to heal naturally.

Kevin gets up and sits with her on the arm of the chair. The two begin to browse the catalogue together. As for Mobbee, he hops off the couch and just about leans over the chair's armrest where he can see the bottom part of the magazine. In his head, Kevin begins to identify different flame magic artefacts like catalysts and wands for stronger pyromancy.

Kevin speaks aloud suddenly. "Why are they advertising tools that make your flame magic stronger when the main source comes from the body, that's so stupid- anyone who's studied it for five minutes would know not to get one. There's like what, *two* spells you can do with a fire wand, and *both* are useless."

Leah replies. "Well at least you don't have to lug a staff and wands around with you to work like I do. It's a package deal for water magic."

Within the pages also lie prices for bulk orders of mana quartz, both extinguished and pre-charged; valuable resource for enchanting jewellery, weaponry and even everyday things. It not only looks pretty but it stores and replicates the charge meaning it rarely ever runs out. Many quality crystals and tools are listed between the pages, but one item sparks the pair's attention.

The book seemed to call out as if it was demanding for Leah to buy the item, a crescent moon charm, detailed with glyphs and patterns that weave all through the piece. *I so need to get this...* she thought to herself. But as she loaded the website on her phone and waited for it to load, it had already been taken; not just one but the only two they had.

"Oh well," Kevin sighed. "It looked mint, but what would you do with it anyway? It doesn't look like it'd work on your regular staves or jewellery. Too chunky in my opinion."

Leah lets out a sad sigh of agreement- the corner of the page still between her fingers waiting to be turned, though her eyes have yet to be gorged by the delicate and valuable charm that the pages tease her with. At last, she strips her gaze from the entwining unobtainable jewel and raises from the floral armchair. She tosses her magazine on the chair from where she sat and stretches her weary arms and legs, letting out a yawn that puts the house to sleep.

Kevin catches her yawn and turns the TV off before putting Mobbee over his shoulder and mumbling out another yawn. "Well, I'm off to bed. I Gotta be up bright-eyed and bushy-tailed tomorrow if I don't want to blow myself up. Heh."

Leah picks up her volume and replies from a small distance as she takes the finished cups and tray into the kitchen to clean them. "Alright, nighty night then. Don't forget to set your alarm!"

Kevin; with the cat in tow marches upstairs holding Mobbee under his arm, feeling the elegantly carved pattern on the wooden railing, the pattern subconsciously reminds him of the charm he saw in the magazine with Leah bare moments ago.

He walks into his room and puts the cat down on his bed, who only jumps off ungratefully to rebound onto his own, pile of cushions at the foot of the bed headfirst. The walls are barely visible, plastered with posters, yet only one holds the privilege of always makes him smile upon seeing it as he wakes and falls. A poster he's had since he was a boy- though torn and battered over time, it still clearly shows his one and only childhood hero, Zapp Susanna Bolt- the Storm Commander. A fierce heroine who tolerates no nonsense from her foes.

Swift as lightning and more powerful than the hammer of Thor, her axe that crashes down from the blackened clouds decides the final verdict of all her foes. On the bottom of the poster lies some faded text that reads, "In your heart, a storm brews. Embrace it and empower the commander within."

Zapp Susanna, though not the leader, is one of the most popular Heroes of the group fittingly named the Advance Heroes. Her can-do attitude and powerful aura inspire the masses. Her battles are a spectacle to behold first hand, watching them on TV simply doesn't cut it for most, though Kevin has never seen her inaction in real-life he has every single one of her battles taped; her style is as brutal as a bear and her speed as quick as lightning.

Aside from his single inspiration, his shelves are stuffed to collapsing with games, memorabilia and rows and rows of books. He's ran out of space on both sets of shelves and has started placing smaller books *in front* of all the others. All are ordered alphabetically and numerically, those without numbers but are part of a set are instead organised into colour.

He nips out of his room and returns after a quick shower to find an already soundly asleep cat, curled up on a mountain of cushions as if he's a dragon protecting his gold. Kevin turns out the lights and zips into bed soundly... Resting up for an exciting day ahead...

The night passes like the earth to the sun as Kevin tosses and turns. The sandman's gag prevents him from waking as his face gains wrinkles from his nocturnal tension. In the deepest stretches of his mind, he sees a light- faded and dull though still trying to shine with all its heart. Its red glow though conforming felt oh so warding; a sense of dread lied behind the light- though he could only walk forward.

A soft voice calls out from the, shining red light. "Find me... Though lose me not again..."

Words bubble out of Kevin's mouth amidst his slumber as if a torrent of water swallowed his very being as the bubbles from his lungs flew to the top. He kicks and splashes in the sea of dreams though to no avail... He springs up at nearly half the speed of sound in a hot sweat. He gathers his head, so he doesn't lose his dream.

Lose me not again... What was that about? He pondered, regulating his breathing as he spun toward the bed's left side.

Kevin wipes the drip from his forehead before standing up and beginning his morning routine. He leaves his room open so Mobbee can wander out and downstairs where he lays out breakfast for him. The bond between them is powerful, and though Kevin doesn't have the time to say goodbye in the morning he makes up for it when he gets back home.

"You're up early," Leah says calmly from behind. "Guess you *are* excited for your field lesson if you're getting up an hour earlier, eh?" She adds, yawning and stretching her arms towards the clouds.

Kevin responds, catching her yawn as usual. “I've gotta get to work either way, don't I? I'm excited but it's like that *bad* kind of excited, y'know?”

Leah gives Kevin a blank, bewildered stare and waits for him to figure out what the words that he spouted meant. As great an educator he may be, he's never been good at describing things; often making uncanny noises and gestures in a feeble attempt to speak his thoughts, though he just ends up looking foolish in the end.

With breakfast skipped, Kevin bids farewell to Leah before speeding off at breakneck speeds, darting through the towns and cities that keep him from his work. Because he can move at Mach speeds without causing damage he usually waits until the last moment before setting off to work. He has all the time in the world and can enjoy his morning before setting off with a blast, though today was different by a long shot from the norm. He woke up early, skipped breakfast and didn't even regulate his kick-off, causing a moderate degree of burns to the road as he ran...

Chapter 2
Sparks of Cinder

Coming to a screeching halt, Kevin arrives at the college long before the nick of time. He walks through the vibrant campus grounds and into the same contrasting uninteresting classroom which sports today's usual daily rigmarole. Morning lessons mostly include English literature, magic theory and a whole lot of paperwork, though today's afternoon will be *very* different.

The time slowly burns away like a candle, and the sun passes through the sky; Its rays beam down on the quiet city as the cold, chilling wind bites bare skin. It's the afternoon now and Kevin has his lunch in the staff room, he looks around the begrimed room to find that Thome is missing.

He always waits here for me... must be in some other room marking those papers... Kevin thinks to himself. As the clock strikes 1PM, Kevin bolts to his classroom, quickly pushing the smoky glass door open, stumbling and losing his balance through his own uncontainable momentum. On the other side sits Thome, marking dozens of worksheets at Kevin's desk, exactly as he thought. Thome doesn't even seem to notice Kevin tumble into the room, he sits on the old, inexpensive chair, scratching his pen onto the papers, ticking, clicking and writing notes...

Kevin stares deeply at Thomes coat. As a higher-up in the college, Thome feels it's his duty to wear fancy custom embroidered cloak to work. It's a pale pear-green piece with embroidery around the hem of the eight elements he wields. Between the calming green and exiting symbols runs maroon swirls in a complex racing pattern, enough to put any beholder in a trance. Once again, he is reminded of that charm he saw in Leah's magazine- its crescent moon shape and its swirling intricate engravings. At once, he snaps out of his daydreaming and grabs Thome's attention with heed and volume.

"Morning, mate! That Autumn weather's getting a bit chilly, isn't it?" He asks, excitement visibly beaming from his smooth baby face.

Thome is genuinely bewildered to see Kevin so happy and full of energy, by Friday the two are usually fed up and ready to fall asleep at any given moment. "Well colour me pink- look who's got some energy for once. You must be ready for the lesson I bet?" Thome puts a question on Kevin's mind.

Kevin swiftly replies. "Methinks I've been too cynical about all this field lesson business. If I'm going to burn something I might as well enjoy it, ey?" He chuckles, grinning widely.

"I can't tell if he's genuinely happy or if he's just gone potty." Thome whispers to Ethos, who rests on the back of the chair, who blips in agreement.

Kevin eagerly awaits at his desk with Thome, kicking his legs back and forth in childlike anticipation, unable to wait any longer- like an egg ready to release its chick into the open world. *Soon... Veeerrrry soon.* He speaks to himself in his own head.

At long last the students poured into the classroom in a hodgepodge of excited and dissuaded faces. Kevin pushes the door closed with the swift, energised shove of his foot and stacks Thome's papers up at blinding speeds into a neat pile. Then, without explaining a single thing to the pupils who haven't even had a chance to sit down, he races outside telling them all to follow along.

The full extent of his excitement had spiked- the classroom door swung open so fast that the hinge seized up- no longer able to close on its own. The open monochrome halls become like that of a spectrum of burning oranges, serine yellows and pure whites, a cacophony of suppressed passion for his work and magic.

He breaks off free from the floor as he darts through the empty halls, his excitement starts to steam out of his mouth like a kettle whistling at the pain of flame; pinballing from wall to wall until he leaps out of the front doors and lands himself in the middle of the field.

Meanwhile back in the classroom, the students have only just started to move sluggishly through the halls as Thome & Ethos take the lead. Ethos swivels through the crowd of young students, springing to life and soaring out of the window to fly after Kevin with an eager twinkle, spinning and throwing herself around as she descends.

The class finds their way outside from within the walls of the small, divided building and all fourteen students arrive in the large open yard. Kevin gets the tiring health and safety spiel out of the way before bellowing to the class, adorned in their orange & coal-black flame-resistant uniform.

“Alright, are you all ready?!” Kevin shouts excitedly.

The eager half of his pupils virtually jump with joy as they pull out spell tomes from an oversized pocket on the inside of their long blazers. Kevin attempts to reassure the other side of the class; still half-asleep, that the lesson will be far more interesting than they think it'll be. He pulls out his own miniature spell book; thick as a brick and flips through the first couple of pages without even looking at the index. He stops on the seventh page and blankly reads the first spell listed.

Though before he asks the students to perform, Kevin recalls an important first step related to casting. He explains to his students the necessity of a warm body or nearby heat source to draw from, though his working ends up being all over the place as usual.

They all look at their equally confused teacher, who had given up trying to verbally explain and instead, began a physical demonstration as Thome explained in his stead.

"As a primary power source, flame magic draws from the heat within the caster. Your uniform is also lined with thermal material which traps heat, equipping you with a secondary source too." He then inquires if everyone feels warm, and much of the class responds with a unanimous, "Yes, sir!"

Clearly to both tutors, it's obvious that Thome has gained the most respect out of the two- despite his skills in this department being inferior to Kevin's. Kevin, looking at his pupils who are now prepared for their chance to perform their first exciting outdoor lesson with him. And after Thome's rally- they assert their confidence in Kevin by lifting their tomes high and paring off.

A final safety precaution is put in place as Thome pulls out a wand with what seems to be blue tape around its black, wooden handle to create several beautiful, glistening, air-suspended water bubbles... just in case.

With all prepared, Kevin demonstrates a simple, classic fireball spell. He presses his hands together tightly and focuses on the body heat within his hands. As his hands begin to build warmth, he pulls them apart to reveal a bright amber ball of blazing gas and light. He begins to wave it around in the air, spinning it rapidly around his arms and body like a professional dancer- until he finally drops the ball of amber deliberately and smoulders it into the mire with his foot.

“Right then, that was a really easy fireball spell, does anyone have any questions?” Kevin asks heartily.

A tall man from the back of the class, no older than eighteen with jet-black hair half shaved with the other half covering his face, raises his hand as fast as a hare in anticipation; waving left to right like a flag in a hurricane. “Sir, could you give us a step by step demonstration as to how to cast the spell?”

“Sure thing. Everyone, follow me as I go!” Kevin promptly repeats the process with intricate step by step instructions. “First of all, close your hands tight, then focus on pushing your magic into the palms of your hands.” He explains as his students and himself perform the intuitive instructions.

Panning around the yard, he sees boys and girls clad in black and orange all with their hands sealed shut with a glowing core, waiting to burst and show off their inner burning talent.

“Keep those hands closed 'til they feel nice and hot... Then pull them apart and show off those colours!”

The eager children with all speed, pull their hands apart one after the other to divulge their embers into the open air. The row of young men and women have created astonishing wisps of ember in their palms from amber to ivory and even rose pink and will-of-the-wisp blue. Though some students fail to ignite a spark, they keep at it, and that's what matters to Kevin; brought to whimpering joy. Holding back tears only a proud tutor could shed. Finally seeing for himself his students' potentials igniting into glorious flames of dignity.

Drying the few tears, he turns to his noble students and applauds them for their efforts; Thome and Ethos can't help but join him in the praise.

“Well done everyone!” Kevin hoots.

“You've truly outdone yourselves! Bravo!” Hails Thome. Ethos' aura changes from pale silver-green to a warm orange colour- mimicking the fire that bewilders her, her aethereal power fairing and flickering like a candle flame.

As the lesson goes on, many spells are cast from the ever-burning paraffin that dwells within the young students. Flames arise from their palms as a ringmaster tames a lion with his whip. Fire rings, will-o-wisps and many more sparks and flairs warm the chilled air around the young men and women.

A few rare talents soar above and beyond expectations by tapping into the aethereal plain, summoning forth the very essence of their deepest aspirations, desires and motives, creating conjures.

Kevin's eyes widen at these freshly born beasts; the fire-like attributes of the fascinating creatures no doubt a trademark of a fire mage's abilities. Some don thick, armoured scales and others have plumes of amber feathers, and some have no fiery attributes at all. He carefully observed the creations who are still confounded from their sudden birth from flame and void.

“Did you know conjures come from the elements of the earth, born from your strongest passions and ideals.” Explained Kevin. “I can see some loyal friends that'll stick with you for the rest of your lives. Take care of them and they'll do the same for you.”

A young lady with hair tied up in a neat ponytail turns to her ecstatic teacher with her new conjure- feathered and flamed as it perches on his shoulder. “Mr. Marrowald, do have any conjures?”

Kevin turns to his young pupil and replies with Elation. “I do, two actually! One's a big wobbly house cat who helps with the chores around the house. The other one... doesn't come out very often.”

“Why is that?” Another pupil asks.

Kevin dissembles his words. “She's uh... too big for the college. She has wings the size of trucks. She's not very friendly either. One time she-”

Though before Kevin could finish his muses, the chill of the day seemed to grow angrier; silencing him and blowing out any fire that had been cast around the college yard.

A whirl and a rumble came from the road just outside the college and shook the earth below. Students and mentors alike bolted out of the college buildings; Kevin being the first to observe the devastating quakes' origin. Though through quick inspection this shock wave had come from a summoning gateway that links a conjure from their purgatorial sleep to the living, waking world.

These gates were not manned by any mage, however. Far too similar to the scenario the news warned about. Though the gate had been stretched open, not a single beast had emerged from its depths.

“Well, this is a strange coincidence. It sure is a big one, do you think its jammed?” Thome asks with clear confusion.

“I don't think it is... Someone would have had to put this here recently, so whoever it is should probably still be nearby.” Replies Kevin cautiously. “Tell everyone to get back inside, we need to have a closer look.”

“Righto Kev! I'll get Christine to come and find you ASAP.” Thome responds and he has the pupils follow him inside.

“And don't call me Kev!” He sighs with his parting words.

With those parting words, Thome escorted the pupils into the building along with Ethos who circled the young students protectively- making sure no harm came to them.

Kevin broke from the path and made his speedy descent down the hill upon which the college is perched. He makes a screeching halt as he comes to a stop; dirt flying from the bottom of his boots that scar the concrete beneath him. The town was on a sudden high-alert lockdown; shops had their shutters down and house doors were locked tight with their nosey inhabitants poking through the curtains. Kevin uses his momentum to give the unattended gate a whooping crack with his knee to shatter it.

Though Kevin kneed it with the power of a mule, the gate roared and rumbled even louder like a hungry dragon scouring for its next gruesome meal. All at once the gate starts to whir and spin, magic energies being engulfed in its vortex before a wolf-like beast of the earth comes rushing out, tackling Kevin to the ground as it shrieks and snarls; a beast like Kevin had never seen before. Promptly gathering heat into his fingertips, Kevin sharply jabs the fowl brute with his hand. He ascends to his feet and enlaces his muscular legs with blaze before cracking the monster with vigorous impact. It howls skyward; its crystalline protrusions glisten magenta and violet before circling Kevin in a blur of light. Standing firm, he waits for the beast to charge. And charge it does with all its might, baring its fangs and whipping its tail as it tears up the brickwork of the ground; It pounces, ready to take a bite out of Kevin.

Like from a horror story, the trees blow violently as Kevin abruptly vanishes into thin air with an ominous boom. The mutt still baring its crystal teeth springs around, sniffing and growling at the singed road. The fragmented spikes on its back pulsing with energy swing around as it turns, searching for its slippery prey. Before long, a flickering light shines from behind the vile creature- Its hair and ears stand on end.

“You know, I'd hoped if I were to be attacked by a conjure today it would of at-least been charming.” Kevin's cocky voice calls to it, mocking its primitive intelligence and beastly manner.

Soon before the brutal behemoth could even register what was going on, a ring of light begins to shine on the ground, symbols and glyphs write themselves around the ghastly conjure as a heavenly glow rushes from the ground below- then *FHOOOOOUUGHHHH* -A brutally tall column of magma and flame sends it flying way up high into the air.

The burned and terrified conjure kicks and yawls as it plummets to the ground, crying out as it crashes down onto the blackened road below; its crystal quills smashing under the impact. It twitches and struggles as its body decomposes into bright, sparkling energy- looking its hunter in the eye with a wicked leer before returning to purgatory.

The streets stay quiet and civilians stare from their hiding places in awe, never before laying witness to such a violent yet captivating display. The gate the beast dwells from cracks and splits; the indigo glow of its whirling vortex comes to a complete stop before shattering like a thin layer of glass. The people throw themselves out of their hiding spots as they all cheer for their saviour. Though their hero is disheartened, unwilling to accept all the attention; overwhelming him, choking him.

As the townsfolk begin to surround Kevin, he turns around to be greeted by Thome who's in frantic discomposure after watching from inside the college walls- joined by the principal with newly tied-up hair and magic embalmed hands.

“Kevin are you okay?!” Christine yodels as she darts her hands towards Kevin, already enhanced with glowing golden magic. “Let me heal you. There, there dear...”

He grimaces as Christine waves her hands around his body, quickly sealing up any cuts and bruises he had gained in the fight with the terrifying felon.

“OW!” He wails, flailing himself around at the sensation of his small wounds being sealed up and healed. “You have any idea how much that stings? I didn't even get hurt in that fight; you're just healing me for the sake of it." He wails and shouts.

Christine shakes her head; she swipes the excess magic energies from her hands with class. "If it stings then you know that it's working now, don't you? you need to accept other people's help when it's given to you. One day you might find yourself in a rough patch where you just can't do it alone~."

Kevin sighs and shrugs off the stinging sensation. "Okay, I don't need another Christine-lecture. I get it... Thanks..."

The three share a moment of respite as they let the ashen clouds settle down. Before long, Kevin pipes up once more. "Oh, uh- about the damages. Don't tell me I have to cover those."

Thome tidies his coat that blew tatty during his hasty jog, he replies as he fixes his collar. "Don't worry, it's only a little bit of road this time. The council needs to fix the paving here anyway, am I right, Grand Mistress?"

"Quite right, Thome!" Christine sings. "The college won't have to fork out of its *already dwindling funds* to fix the mess. The important thing is that the damages are minimal; only some wobbly pavement and singed road. Nothing the council won't fix... When they can be bothered to that is! Oho-oh-oh-oho~!"

Thome and Kevin both snicker at Christine's cheap dig at the town council's incompetence- but Kevin can't shake the abnormal pit in his stomach... An impending feeling grows in his gut- growing and expanding like a moth from a cocoon.

The pit grows larger, engulfing all serenity until Kevin finally speaks. “That's probably not the only gate.”

Thome turns to Kevin; his laughter quickly shattered. “What do you mean?”

Kevin replies. “That gate I shut down shouldn't be the only one. It's never just the one with these kinds of things, there's always more.”

“As much as I hate to admit- your intuition usually isn't wrong.” Speaks Thome, gripping his bag in anticipation.

“We should definitely look around for more gates. I don't like having to work overtime.” Kevin casts a sickle of flame into his hand- dragging his fingers swiftly through the air, drawing its nature into being. He snatches it from the air, wielding it as if it were a short sword with ember that flickers around its surface.

“Right then,” Christine adds. “I'll call the Advance Heroes right away. Everyone will be as safe as can be under the watch of you two!” With her leaving speech, Christine runs off as fast as her squatty legs can carry her to get back into the college.

The wind in tandem with the people of the town grows quiet, as soft as a wisp of silk. Nothing but a soft breeze, barely enough to blow your hair. Kevin and Thome walk together in tense silence, spell book and sickle in hand. The only sound they make is the tapping of their shoes on the road.

The silence shatters; Thome begins to speak with pep. “It's sort of convenient that these gates opened during a practice lesson. Now you can show your pupils all the explosions you want from a much safer distance. They can see from the classroom windows well I bet.”

Kevin turns his head to Thome, returning the conversation. “It's inconvenient too- I was beginning to have fun until these conjures called for an interruption.”

Thome chuckles. “Lighten up a little. There's no need to be such a stick in the mud, is there? You're usually the calmest person I know, if not conspicuously cocky.”

“You're right, it's not like me at all. I just don't like going out of my way to sort this kind of thing out. It's my lesson though and I've been put in a bad mood so at this point I'm just using it for stress relief.”

The two slow down their march for a while so Kevin can catch his breath. Though speeding at Mach-7 takes no effort, fighting and teaching exhaust him quite swiftly. They keep walking with haste as Thome tucks away his spell book. Ethos, ready for action, starts to spiral around Thome in an atomic pattern whilst chirping and whizzing.

As they walk, Kevin's mind begins to freeze and slip deep into his subconscious. His thoughts float in the cloudy abyss of his inner well as a woman in red wielding a short sword dances around gracefully, creating ribbon-like trails with the deadly dance of steel- smiting the same beast he had just bested on his own. When Kevin reignites his attention, he finds himself with Thome and Ethos, standing in front of another gate.

“Well then, looks like we found one, are you ready?” Asks Thome, levitating a catalyst of earth above his head, its geometric frame revolving around a golden core. He attempts to resonate with the summoning gate- placing his hand before it, though not touching its mystical aether... The gate reacts not to his call.

“Maybe I should use a different element...” Ponders Thome with a befuddled look, cycling through the thick pages of his custom-made tome.

In advance of Thome casting a different element, Kevin steps forward towards the gate; still as a rock. A cast of orange embers swirls around his arm as he rotates his wrist and gathers it to his hand- thrusting it forwards towards the gate at high speeds. The orb of blaze rockets down the cold tarmac road, warming the air around it as a campfire would to a lonely traveller.

The burning aether splashes against the gate in a flowering pattern of crimson and amber. Like before, the gate begins to shine- glyphs begin to form around its many rings whilst the many shapes swirl around it like a group of dancers.

“That's so strange...” Thome wonders to himself. “How come it only activated when you cast a spell at it?”

“Because they don't like your audacity. Anyway, this one's all you, knock yourself out man!” Kevin replies.

“Very well, Marrowald. Watch and learn how the Multi Mage does things!”

As the gate sparkles and spins a pair of glaring, dotted eyes stretch out of the aether rings, pulling out a long leathery body. The eyes spring out of the conjure's head like slinky toys. Its snake-like body flairs with the fury of lightning, jittering and zapping out of control. The yellow beast swings its noodle-like eyes around like huge whips, suddenly freezing their movement altogether as they lock onto Thome.

The two stare each other down with the intent to attack. Kevin takes an inhumanly large boost-hop backwards, placing his trust in Thome's strength and skill. The snake-like beast circles itself before rocketing into the air with its eyes rotating around its head, one each locked onto Samuel and his conjure. As it swishes and flicks its enormous tail, more of its body is eaten by sparks of thunder, shaking and zipping like a plasma ball.

The dragon lunges with the rage of a bull at most, though is foiled by Thome who hastily rolls to the right, crouching after his roll and swinging his enlaced arms which launch boomerangs of wind at the reptilian titan. The spinning slings lands at the conjure's tail, blowing away a burst of sparks and cutting its flesh, revealing a yellow scaly body beneath its raging lightning.

The sly serpent sucks in its eyes like a snail, the eyes glow a pure blinding white; brighter and brighter they glow as they retract into the monster's head. A splitting flash fills the air as the town around them becomes monochromatic, the light tightens into a nova-hot beam, chasing Thome down as he promptly runs from the volatile heat. The black-haired hero raises his hand; Ethos flies to his aid in no time and changes her aura to that of a gritty, dusty brown, throwing herself directly in front of the deadly lasers. Her perfectly round body expands into a sheet that flicks the death-dealing beams away like flies.

Thome calls Ethos to his side and her body quickly snaps back to its regular round shape, hovering to his shoulder as he charges up a jade green essence around his arms, the ground beneath the battle begins to rumble and quiver, though the horrible ochre beast refuses to yield. It takes to the skies spiralling higher and higher until it locks onto Thome once more. A final attack; lunging all its weight at Thome and Ethos from altitudes on high.

The black-haired mage throws his elbows back, drawing an arch of green and silver leaving his entire chest exposed to any incoming attacks. the wind kicks up, with his fists held back he calls upon the galling power within, forming into a rushing blackhole of hurricanes combined.

The beast's mind shatters as the mint coat-wearing mage propels his fists forwards, bombing the hurricane orb directly at the caitiff. Its thunder stroke aura is swallowed by the vacuum as its body is twisted and shredded, its head being slapped against the ground as it spins and whirls, leaving only fragments of its body in Thomes wake.

The beasts dismembered segments melt into yellow crystalline dust, unfurling and evaporating in a spark-like way- shredding its ethereal form and vanishing back to the pool of magic and mana from where all conjures are born.

Thome shakes the wind magic from his enchanted arms, flying off in a thousand shades of avian colours. He congratulates Ethos for her contribution by flipping a treat her way- catching it mid-air. He rubs her cheek gently as she spins around before wriggling her way back into Thome's bag to rest and meld against his cluttered belongings. He dusts off his coat and turns to Kevin with his fists on his hips in celebration.

“See, that's the power of Carvina's legendary Multi Mage!” He gloats with a smug grin.

Kevin walks over to Thome slowly and returns the conversation. “You used one element- your title doesn't really work here.”

Thome replies. “Yes, but one was all I needed! Perhaps you should brush up on your catalyst training before you criticize my own magic, Kev.”

Kevin swings his head to the left, shying away from the wounding observation; looking a tad self-conscious. “Just to learn how to change the shape of a flame that's only burning on inorganic materials? No thanks...” He scoffs, walking away.

Thome dusts himself off from the dirt, dust and debris again and quickly scrambles towards Kevin, dropping pages and books from his overstuffed pochette. “Hey-where are you going? Mistress Christine said we've got to stay together!” He screams about their separation.

Though Thome's calls reach Kevin's ears, he doesn't wave his ground. Not wanting to listen to more of Thome's gloating, the fire wielder keeps his intrepidity and carries on his search for another gate...

Chapter 3
The Crimson Blade

After a long day of blowing smoke and fire around its now finally Saturday, a day where he can finally kick his feet up and cuddle with Mobbee while reading a good book whilst enjoying a cup of milky tea, and he does just that. He opens his arms in bliss and lazily flops back onto the sunken couch with the old book that he was reading yesterday in class.

He wiggles and shimmies into the cushions of the sofa and pets Mobbee's silver fur. He lets out a long, peaceful yawn as he opens the thick pages of his book. Mobbee doesn't properly understand what Kevin's saying but he still listens to the story anyway; curled up like a cinnamon roll.

— *The Queen of red, sitting upon the bloodstained throne listened to her kingdom's uproar- her soul begins to rattle from the sound of the angry people outside the castle walls, her temper boiling up. They scream, they shout, and they demand to see the Traitor Queen. They demand to know what her true intentions are for their kingdom and country. She places her elbows upon the arm of the bloody throne and strokes her pointed ears; drooping down in silence.* —

— *Her pale hands squash her cheeks as her breath sharpens, sighing and grumbling, trying to find the words to smite her new people with so heavily. Grumbling in the lifeless, empty room; her legs kicking back and forth whilst staring blankly at the ichor-stained floor; she stands at last. She walks from the throne towards the balcony, throwing the curtains behind her. She stands atop the fort of misfortune and stands with her eyes glowing with wicked confidence. —*

— She raised her pale hands high above her pointed ears as she tossed a bright shining beacon into the air, collecting the raging men and women's attention for miles upon miles. They stand from across the old city to the green countryside, staring at the glimmering spark of doom. The Queen parts her lips and calls to the people. "You are all now my slaves- my rule is absolute, yet fair. Not one soul shall leave this kingdom unless it is to fight on behalf of my glory. If you worms will not comply, then this beacon of hells wrath shall drop, rendering your families, children and homes to smoulders." —

— The roaring crowd that was hushed seconds before began to rumble the very earth once more at their inescapable looming threat. Screams and cries alike set the kingdom ablaze. swept over the kingdom as the Queen looked on from the balcony. Just as the damned people thought to act, light shone from the heavens; her five enforcers stood tall on the turrets of the castle. —

— A merciless swordswoman whose hair dripped red with the essence of her fallen victims. —

— A songstress of the lake whose voice held the power to curse the spirits. —

— A doctor whose poisons so potent they harboured the power to kill a god. —

— A silent wizard whose power raged so violently; he could render any living creature to ash. —

— And the leader of the wicked enforcers, A golden lady whose blinding power shone brighter than the sun. —

— The Queen leers down 100ft to see her enforcers pacifying the raging townsfolk and carrying them off into a pile... Freedom had never been further from reach. —

The novel closes, and Kevin sticks a piece of torn paper between the pages as a makeshift bookmark, every bookmark he has ever owned somehow disappears. Where do they go, the shadow realm? One of the many mysteries of the world... Mobbee unfurls from his comfortable position to prod his head against Kevin's arm, then pawing at the book adorably.

“I'll read you some more later, bud.” Kevin says to his cat in a gentle voice.

He slides the aged book onto the coffee table, hooking his mug with his fingers and takes a long sip of tea before placing it down. As the mug taps the oak table, Leah walks in with her own cup of coffee and a fresh magazine with newer magic trinkets inside. She sits down next to her brother, propping her legs up on the table as they squish Mobbee between each other, which he doesn't seem to mind.

The magazine flips open and the pages spin to the enchantment section. Her mind instantly begins to sink into the book as she gazes over each item and their great details. Fire crystals, thunder bangles, raw magic enhancers- the new volume has it all.

“Hey, it's that moon-looking thing again.” Kevin points out. “What does it say under it?”

Leah responds, reading the details. “It looks like an Ad. It says, 'A rare crescent amulet of Silvalish origins. This item is being recalled due to unsafe properties.' It has a return address too, but it's not a UK address. That post code's enormous." Leah groans.

"That doesn't even look like an Earthy post code. Maybe it's a post code from Silvalon?"

"Maybe... I'll check later, though." She responds, glaring at the reflective pages.

The silence of reading grows tranquil as the siblings sit in peace and quiet. What once was 8AM had dragged on to 11. The two were reading the magazine for hours before Kevin realised, he had a huge list of missed calls from Thome on his phone, a sudden sense of urgency drives him to ring Thome back to see what's up. His phone rumbles twice before Thome picks up.

Kevin begins to speak. "Hey, you know I have do-not-disturb on for the weekend, right? What's up-"

Before Kevin can breathe after his sentence, Thome screams down the phone so loud that it spooked Mobbee off the sofa, causing the poor wobbly cat to hit the floor with a soft and airy plop.

Thome bellows "What the hell is wrong with you- how do you miss fourteen calls?! You know some loony has been summoning conjures left and right for the past few days now. They could appear in Lalstrun and you're too busy watching TV to even care!"

Kevin catches his breath and pushes the microphone inward towards his mouth which made him more muffled, but just a bit louder to keep his voice down.

"First of all, *pal*, I was reading a magazine, *not* watching TV. Second, I'm not legally obligated to deal with these kinds of things like you and Christine are- because unlike you two, my magic license is still under oversight. Besides, you're more than capable, so leave me alone or-"

"So let me get this straight," Thome interrupts garish. "Unmanned conjures could be coming to your town of thirty people or less, to rip all the little cottages to shreds and you'd just sit there with your nose stuffed in a brick of paper?!" Thome retaliates.

Progressively getting more agitated at Thome's logic, Kevin's coy tone turns to an angry graze as he walks outside to talk in the front garden with his phone still pressed heavily to his mouth. "Now you're twisting the situation. You know that if I join in when I'm off duty I could get in seriously deep shit. I'm not allowed to use disruptive magic outside of my working hours. And if, *and I mean a BIG IF* they came to Lalstrun then I'd deal with them quickly before anyone got hurt. You know that."

Thome barks back. "Oh, well I am *so sorry* that I'm ruining your lovely peaceful weekend. Do carry on lazing the hours away while that big purple demon-dog from yesterday comes to rip your legs off. Ta-ta Kev!"

"Stop calling me Kev you-" **click* * -The phone falls silent. "-Knob..." and to Kevin's dismay, his last laugh had been stripped away from him yet again.

Opening the door behind Kevin, Leah comes outside just to the doorstep to see what her brother was shouting about- who's breathing heavily as he contemptuously stuffs his phone into his pocket. "What was all that?" She asks, peeping from behind the front door. "You're going to have the neighbours complaining about the noise again."

Kevin puffs a deep breath. “Thome being a cocky knob as per usual that's what. 'Oh~ I doth be so inclined to apologize that oneself be ruining your weekend, however, there doth be a large purple ugly beast racing towards your own lodging, of which is the face-ripping kind. ***TATA.***'” He mocked blaringly.

Trying not to laugh at Kevin's scarily accurate mockery of Thome, her attention is brought to the conjure that Kevin mentioned. “You said 'racing towards our own house' right? And it's the- uh... 'face ripping' kind?”

“There was a ta-ta at the end, Leah.”

“What's that quickly approaching t-thing in the distance, then!?”

Leah questions shakily while peering to the right of the road pointing at a jagged silhouette bumping up and down on the road as it glides down the cobble and dirt path of the quiet countryside village.

Kevin turns to where his sister was pointing; squinting at the thing she seems so panicked about, yet he brushes it off as unimportant. “It's probably just the milk truck doing its early rounds, why are you panicking-”

But yet again, Kevin had been interrupted by another rude and loud force, a roaring beast scratches its claws into the gravel pathway. The same demonic monster towers over Kevin once more as it lets out a blood-curdling howl. Teeth gnash with a thirst for blood and claws grip the earth. The garden fence and nameplate had been mostly ripped down by the monsters grinding halt.

Leah begins to panic, desiring to run to Kevin's aid, yet hiding behind the door, shuddering and barely able to speak. “Yes, there is a reason to panic! Get rid of that thing- I don't know what it is but I want it out of my garden now!!"

"Oh. Magic man wasn't kidding." Kevin gulps.

He solemnly peers up at the blackened beast, observing its chest. It has scratches and marks from when he used Ember Jab on it before, which puzzled him greatly; he muses to himself- *Conjures aren't supposed to have scars...* He raises his gaze to the beast's vile mug, its black ridged snout covered in laced, amethyst-like protrusions; and he says one thing while giving a cheeky smile.

"Nice to see you again, ugly!" He remarks, hiding a smirk behind his curly blonde locks. The beast; though it doesn't understand Kevin's words, raised a brow in question; jumping and snapping at him, seeing only small prey within claws' reach. Suddenly its bristly mane rustles up; a pale purple glow emerges from the wolf's mane, then a pair of large curly antennae, *then* a yellow orb-like creature donning dazzling, lavender butterfly wings with a voice shriller than the screech of a parrot.

"WHO ARE YOU CALLIN' UGLY THEN!!?" The creature screeches in a wild, high-pitched voice. Lips stretching and face contorting like a cartoon character at the surprising volume the small creature booms.

"Uh, who are you supposed to be?" asks Kevin, completely bewildered by this quite surreal experience.

"Who are you shuposhed t' be?" The creature mimics back at him, jeering at his accent and googling its dotted eyes around. The round one starts to wretch at Kevin for seemingly no reason, making vile faces at him in a viciously mocking manner. She then rolls over on the

wolfs back, slapping her wings against the beast she sits atop as she cackles and chuckles.

Leah, hiding behind the door, whispers to Kevin. "*What's up with that conjure- why's it so weird?"*

The creature goes wide eyes and snaps back to him faster than lightning. "OY OY OY!!" It shrieks with great angst. "I ain't some *smelly little conjure-* I'm Reegie! *REEGIE!!* And I know who you are, Narrowball. You're that-horrible, *nasty,* ***BAD GUY-*** who beat up my master's favourite puppy!"

Kevin pipes up. "It's Marrowald, not Narrowball, and- 'Bad guy?!' I was defending myself against that tosspot you call a puppy. That thing attacked me first-"

"AR-AR-AR-ARRRRRH SHUDDUP. I talk first- listen, you've been horrible to my master's doggy-doo and now it's time to pay the price!" She growls and screams at Kevin, making his poor ears buzz with pain as she mimics her ferocious companion.

The wolf of doom roars high, filling the air with a satanic wave of despair that makes the very sky a shroud of darkness. Leah unsteadily grabs her staff from behind the door; throwing it to Kevin from across the garden with her quivering hands. He catches the staff and points its lapis lazuli edge at the demon dog, doing so until he notices its lapis core.

"What are you doing Loo? I can't use this- it's an aqua staff-" He explains.

She quivers and twitches in response. "J-Just hit it or something, if you break it, I'll just buy another one- just make those bloody things go away!"

Kevin puffs out a sigh as he turns toward Reegie and her master's beastly conjure. “I tried to teach puppers some tricks the last time we met but it clearly doesn't learn very well. You should try to teach it how to fetch instead!!” He claps his hands together and lobs a searing hot molten ball at the pair of mystic beasts like a meteorite dodgeball.

The devil grips the ground with its gargantuan onyx claws, scraping gashes into the soil as it glides back from the collision- taking the blow to its face, staring Kevin down with its blade-like indigo gaze through the clearing smoke.

Leah calls out with great angst- “Stop taunting the thing and get rid of it!”

“Fine.” He replies, prancing towards the monsters. He leaps into the air and slaps the oceanic staff around the earthly creature's head so hard that the white oak & quartz spine shattered into splinters from the impact, shattering the left side of the diabolical hound's face, hollow as the void, crumbling within itself through the velocity of the whooping crack. Kevin barely lands himself on two feet due to the sheer speed.

Even so, the wolf stole itself, stood with its friend latching onto its grey-haired neck. The canine yelps as it stands, baring its dripping fangs, the right size of its muzzle showing its void like throat and seething black tongue. Noticing that Kevin is still gathering his focus the moth-like creature, Reegie, bids the beast to launch itself directly at Kevin's home, where his defenceless sister and conjure stood instead.

The world in his eyes immediately turns grey as he turns; leering at the impending doom the hellhound ought to bring. Time seems to stop altogether as the picture of a monstrosity inches away from taking a bloody chunk out of his only families face settles in his mind. The sudden realisation and the sight of Leah's petrified look lit a familiar spark of power in his soul.

A flash shone above his crown of golden locks; like the wind, he dashed and gripped the beast by its sharply bristled, bushy tail. The idle soul awakens bellow the dripping blood from his punctured hands; hurling the entire monster over his head, separating the two for half a mile as Reegie bowls down the lane while smashing the fence. The butterfly fled in a panicked state, though Kevins eyes were only set on the large, hollow creature.

His once gentle emerald-green eyes blazed like an angry sun, searing into the devil's heart with a personal vengeance, protecting all that he holds dear. The role of the beast seemed to have reversed as quick as lightning.

He swings the twitching beast into the sky and bows to the floor to leap into the heavens in a flaming aura, which bestowed upon him the gallant wings of the phoenix. A crown of flame is born around his head, flickering under the G-force of his bound. The sky trembles as the ground rumbles; the wolf catches but a blinding glimpse of the exalted winged figure.

An echo from the past sends waves of emblazed power throughout the valley that nearly shatters the ground below, and the shadow of a time long passed compels Kevin's lips to call a voice that is not his own; the same words that cursed the Pale Prince himself.

"BURN UNDER THE WRATH OF SOL!"

The bellow echoes through the valley; shattering the boundaries of the astral laws; a new sun had risen between the ties of fate. Apologies of a regretful, savage scoundrel were whimpered as omnipotent eyes blasted a blinding light that impaled straight through the mutt; the scourge was destroyed in a molten blast, cinder raining down from the sky as Leah stood in awe, but also terror. His blazing wings guide him gracefully down to earth, extinguishing as he stumbles down.

Upon impact, the flaming feathers fall to ashes as he clumsily hits the ground, gasping for air. His frantic sister rushes to his side to help him up. Holding him up off the ground- she feeds a gentle turquoise water magic through her hands and into his chest to recover his drained energy.

"W-what- I-" Leah fumbles her words, unable to roll them off her tongue. "Kevin what- what was **that?!"** She fumbles again, her mind still racing, refusing to grasp what her eyes just captured.

He replies winded and exhausted, his breath as sharp as steel. "I *huff* don't really *wheeze* know-"

"Just hang tight, okay? I'll heal you up and call Christine, she should know what to do."

Yet, stubborn golden-crowned man resists his sister's distraught attempt at assistance. "Look, see?" He beckons while shakily rising to his feet, even though his legs were barely strong enough to hold him upright. "I'm fine, I can- *pant* I can walk, see?" He adds, his lungs still struggling to take in any air as he stumbles back down onto the ground.

Upon realising his master was struggling yet again, Mobbee flung himself out of the house and ran as fast as he could on all fours whaling "Dada, dada!"

“Why do you have to be so headstrong all the time,” Scolds Leah. “One day you're going to need my help major big time and turn it down, then who knows what will happen to you?” Scorns Leah. “And look above your head, you've still got fire over it. Swipe it off already you're wasting your energy!”

Kevin feebly moves his hand over his head and swipes to call off the halo of flames, though his hand passes straight through it as if it were in the realm of illusion. He tries again, sternly swooshing his already exhausted arms, calling nearby flames to his palms to quell them all at once... still nothing. “Well, that's not good...” He remarks.

Leah takes a few steps closer to him. “Here, let me try.” She reaches into her pocket and pulls out a retractable wand, the handle is made of the same haunting white oak her now shattered staff was made from; the retractable part being built from steel pieces. Concentrating, her brow furrows and raises as she flicks her hand in a circular motion thrice.

The water from within the air forms a tennis ball-sized bubble, glistening against Kevin's burning halo. Moving the wands greyish tip towards his halo, pushing the sparkling teel ball over Kevin's head. Then, **Sploosh!!** a sudden drop in the blink of an eye completely drenching his hair, back & jacket.

“OI!” He squeals like a child. “Why'd you have to piss me wet through like that!?”

“Think of it as revenge for my staff. At least that halo's gone now.”

Leah crouches down and summons a teel-green light onto her fingertip. The light glows brighter and brighter until it drips from her finger like water, splashing against the singed ground, opening a faintly glowing area around Kevin and Leah with a refreshing atmosphere. A soothing feeling washes through their veins, like a warm bubble bath. Though suddenly, the crown reignites above his head with an audible gust and scorching burst of heat.

Kevin gazes above his head and sees the feathering amber lights, he sighs as Leah once again drops another blob of cold water on his head... and it comes back once more. Leah groans aggressively as she then holds a ball of water on her brother's head for an extended period, and yet somehow the strange properties of the nimbus allow it to stay lit underwater. “Oh, come on!” Leah grumbles.

The two try a whole manner of things like holding a cold bag of peas on his head and making him drink something cold, yet nothing works. The siblings keep spit-balling ideas until Thome arrives with one familiar, and one not-so-familiar face. As Thome and his unknown friend greet the two siblings, Ethos takes a liking to the flame above Kevin's noggin- so much so that she sits on his head, purring and chirping, mimicking the flame's colours.

“Having fun playing fire fighters, you two?” Thome chuckles.

“Shut up Sam, I'm not in the mood...” Kevin barks back. Upon his closer inspection, Thome's uninvited guest has stout pointy ears and a rather pale, waxy completion. A mercural, for sure.

The extremely casually dressed, green-haired woman introduces herself. “Hiya! The names Diane, or Jackie- just call me DJ; much easier! How's things, guys?”

Kevin answers cynically. "Things are peachy. ...and uh, nice to meet you I guess."

The peppy girl replies. "Nice to meet ya too. Sam here dropped me a call and said he might need help getting rid of a conjure, but it looks like you've done it all by yourself; impressive! What's with the all-powerful, godly halo anyway? Is that a human thing?" She asks as she fiddles with a chunky pair of headphones that lie around her neck.

Leah turns to the new mercural girl and answers for her exhausted brother. "Far from it. We've tried loads of things, like dumping water on his head which at the time- was pretty funny, but it didn't do anything. It feels like we've tried everything. I called Christine, how come she sent Sam instead?"

As he puffs up his chest with a deep breath, the sibling's eyes drop, subconsciously knowing Thome's about to start raising himself on his high horse. "Well, due to me having the multiment it's only natural that she'd send me in her stead. After all, the wonderful lady is a very busy one at that. Her schedule is unfortunately all spent up being Carvina's lead scout. The monsters there weren't so tough anyway; we had it under control from the very beginning thanks to my magical prowess!"

"Cool... I'm guessing you were too busy gloating that you just decided to let those two slips?" Leah replies knowing from experience that if she let him continue, he'd spend the next two hours explaining how *great* he is.

Thome turns his nose up at Leah, with nothing left to say. DJ steps in in his stead. "Well, that wolf was 100% a conjure, there's no questioning that. But the moth- I ain't so sure. I come from Crimson in Silvalon, I've been living here pretty much since the first World Gate was fixed up and I've gotta say, it doesn't look like any conjure I've seen before. We're still workshopping it, Thome'll get back to ya both if we think of something."

"Great- well I'm gonna go and overdose myself on some painkillers. You guys have fun." Kevin remarks as he rolls out of Leah's healing aura. "I ache like mad after fighting that stupid dog again." *And they might just numb my mind enough so that I don't have to listen to the master of murmuring nonsense.*

He gets up and walks through the tidy cottage and plods his way to the bathroom. Kevin looks at his face in the mirror and opens the cabinet, inside sit many boxes and bottles of toothpaste, ibuprofen, paracetamol, aspirin and lots of plasters and bandages.

He picks up a bottle; a deep, almost opaque shade of blue, showing only the small rattling capsules inside as black dots. Turning the white child-proof lid, he takes two painkillers and drinks water directly from the tap to help swallow them. He fills the sink and finally has a chance to think about what happened when he was attacked by that conjure again.

How did it know where I live, and what was that moth thing with it? And why did I get that sudden burst of energy? These questions bounce around in his mind like pinballs in a rubber room. Taking a deep breath in with his shaking hands pressed on the sides of the sink, he throws his head down into the sink of cold water- rubbing his face clean.

As he cleans his face, an echo of an accented voice caresses his submerged ears. "Seek *what we lost all those years ago, lest everything remain obscure..."* A voice speaks to him, brazen with a silky accent. He looks around, was it a prank? Surely if it was, someone would be in the house and not outside. Not in the mood for practical jokes- he searches high and low, around all the doors and in all the wardrobes, yet nobody was hiding anywhere. Peering through the window he could see Samuel, and Leah outside, chatting the day away whilst DJ played with Mobbee and Ethos in the garden...

You're just tired. He tells himself. *There's nobody here but you... just breath...* And that's exactly what he does, taking a long, full breath in with his eyes closed, exhaling through his nose. He opens his eyes and chokes on his breath, as a pale skinned, ruby-haired woman *slides* straight past the living room door frame.

“OY!” he cries out, sprinting through the living room. He looks to the left. *There was somebody there I'm sure- That dancing woman I saw in my dream...* He murmured. He clenches his fists balled in flame, cautiously walking around the house one more time whilst tipping every room upside down to search for this woman he was so sure he saw. Yet nobody turned up at all, not even a bug.

He walks back to the bathroom holding his head, now booming with a dizzying sensation. He turns to look in the mirror to check on his complexion, perhaps he really *was* sick after the fight. Perhaps he'd started to turn pale from all the stress and maybe he needed to lie down... He pulls himself away from the mirror and turns to his bedroom to rest.

And that's when he sees her again, clad in torn red robes with a regal blue lacing- her hair rough and stained in a colour indescribable. Her fierce eyes gaze through his very soul as she stands mere centimetres from him.

He shrieks and grabs the nearest thing and swings it at her at lightning speed, a bottle of shampoo, flinches for a second as he lets go. When he opened them once more the lady had dissipated from his sight, and the bottle stood where it was before he lobbed it. At this point, Kevin begins to freak out-

Crazy ghost ladies, teleporting things?! What the hell is going on?! Only a slither of the finest red silk from her already ruined garments remained on the vivid carpet. A scarlet cutting of ribbon with a finely embroidered moon on it... almost like new. His lungs were now racing- his heart pounding. He wasn't seeing ghosts, was he? Why was everything around him acting so out of sorts? Under all the fear and confusion- Leah's voice barely manages to meet his startled ears.

"Kevin, are you alright in there? I heard you scream- is everything okay?"

Though he didn't respond- not even a peep. Swiping the strange red silk from the floor, Kevin ran from the house, stumbling and tripping, trying to spark his God-Speed to get away from everything he just saw as swiftly as possible. He pushes past Leah, not even noticing her by the front door as he rockets straight past DJ and Thome without even giving them a second glance.

Stumbling down the road faster than a train, he runs to the grove just west of his home- Flogging Woods. Finally gaining some decent footing, he kicks off from the ground properly and speeds through the woods with a resounding *BA-FOOM*, smoky footprints left in his wake as the gangly trees beat and wallop him in the face and chest.

Though his head may be racing, he subconsciously remembers the times he, Leah and their grandma would

walk through these woods on their way home from school- picking up sticks along the way to throw on the fire when they got home, and he remembered the fond times where he lit the fire himself with his magic...

He slows down, his heartbeat calming- at last he stops at a familiar place from a childhood long passed: a small stream with a quaint, little rocky waterfall pouring into it, filtered by small shiny pebbles at the bottom.

He breaths in and catches his long-exhausted breath, taking in the scent of the thicket and the very essence of nature in through his nose and out through his mouth; he repeats this a few times before sitting indolently on a fallen tree to his right; solemnly looking at his reflection in the calm, rippling water... "It's still not gone... why won't it go away?" He whimpers.

Diving deeper into thought, he remembers running away in terror from his mother when she decided to be in one of her volcanic moods- he'd always run back to this same place every time. He and Leah would always sit here by this tranquil stream, throwing pebbles in the water to see who could get the biggest splash whilst their mother calmed down.

He remembers trying to catch fish with his hands, even though he'd always miss. It was this very place where he suddenly unlocked his Hyper-Real power, too. His wretched mother; chasing him down the path as he fled deep into the woods- slowly gaining on him like a lion to its prey.

But within a fingertip's reach something sparked within Kevin's soul; the spirits had given him the chance to save himself and flee faster than the wind to the safe space that only he and his sister knew about. A spark is all it took beneath his feet and before either of them knew it, he had blasted into the woods before his mother could even take a swing at him, knocking her on her arse.

Winding further into the thicket of memories- he remembers first discovering this peaceful grove. He and his grandma were walking home from school on the day of Leah's birth. He recalls it being a dim and rainy day, the downpour rocketing from the clouds on high as if the gods were mourning.

The two of them lost their way within the woods and found themselves at this very flume. The calming vibes the area gave off drowned out the sound of thunder and violent rainfall, and the two sat under a tree on this same fallen log. Gangly branches hung over them with canopies of leaves sheltering the boy and his elder from the storm.

He resurfaces from his memory pool and smiles to himself with his head down, staring at the still waters, not a single ripple in sight. He reflects this upon himself and finally begins to relax...

plop A few ripples run along the top of the waters gently running surface, hitting the edges of the land and dispersing as quickly as they came. He looks up and sees a red, wooden bobber floating in the water; makeshift from carved wood. In the corner of his eye, he catches some thin fishing wire attached to a shabby-looking hand-made fishing pole.

Turning to his left sits a young man clad in old dark green clothing. He has long and scruffy dark blonde hair mostly tucked underneath a maroon hat with a comically sized, rusty bronze bell on the end. Accompanied by a red rope sack with lots of coloured square patches of sewn into it as if it had been torn and punctured many times before.

Kevin didn't have the energy to jump out of his skin again, he was too mentally exhausted. It's almost as if every time he tries to relax something new jumps out at him- never giving him a rest. He gives the boy a short side-eye before dropping his head back down to look at the fish swimming gracefully in the water. His face was that of a young teenager, a clear complexion- only a few dirty smudges on his cheeks and chin.

“I didn't want to disturb you.” Speaks the boy; a tone soft as the shady treetop sun. “I was going to ask if I could join you, but you looked lost in thought.”

Kevin lifts his head and replies. “I've just been thinking about stuff, it'll work itself out... I come here when I feel burned out.”

“I see.” The boy replies politely. “I walk by here to go to my favourite fishing spot; I've passed you a handful of times looking tense, but these clear waters seem to calm you down. My favourite spot was occupied today so I came here instead. You look like you could use someone to talk to. -Would you like a snack?” He asks Kevin happily.

“Uh- thanks, what do you have?” He replies, attention now focused on the kind boy's offering.

The boy holds his fishing pole between his thighs as he reaches down for his thinly wearing bag. He pulls open the top with two fingers and puts it back down on the ground, the opening pointing in Kevin's direction. Inside are random things like a little brass pocket watch, a small leather journal, and a clear flask of water.

The boy closes and shakes the bag to rearrange its contents, the items he saw just a few seconds ago had become buried in fruits and cakes: two stained jars filled with berries, nets of pears and oranges piled up, and cakes wrapped in brown paper bags; cream and jam galore! "Help yourself to anything, a snack always brightens my mood whenever I feel under the weather." The kind angler boy offers.

Kevin replies as he takes a cake with a childlike smile on his face; his sweet tooth has now awoken! "Thanks, mate I appreciate it."

The boy whisks an apple and takes a bite, making a loud crunch. Kevin takes a bite from his cake, and his face was as sparkling and gleeful as ever before- never in so long had he ever tasted a cake as good as this one. He takes another huge bite, spilling an almost glittering purple jam down his shirt, not even caring about the mess he's making.

The boy turns, a smile behind his long caramel hair. "Looking at your face I'd say you're enjoying that?"

"This is the best cake I've had in YEARS. Where did you buy these?" Asks Kevin, giddy with delight.

"Buy them?" The boy questions, only to then answer himself. "I baked them myself, I always carry a few with me- I'll be sure to give you another if I have the time to make some more. That jam is a tricky one to get right." He says in a velvet-like manner, picking up his rod once more and focusing on the pond again. "I believe there's an old human saying- 'A problem shared is a problem halved.' So, if you don't mind my asking... What's been troubling you, friend?" He asks Kevin, who was just about to finish his cake off, licking his fingers clean from the sugary coating. After wiping his mouth with the paper bag, Kevin clears his throat and speaks.

“You've heard about the conjures that have been appearing all around the place, right? They've been turning up everywhere and nobody can figure out who's behind it. Yesterday I had a scuffle with one and today it came back to fight me today with some weird talking butterfly-football thing. I didn't even think about it but now that I have, I wanna know how it even found my house in the first place.”

The boy replies, making sure Kevin had finished as to not be impolite. “Have you considered there could be somebody at work who may be targeting you? I remember as I was walking down to my fishing spot, that's when I saw the sky turn white in the blink of an eye with a loud thundering roar. Does that relate to you?”

Kevin holds his head trying to remember, but his mind is as blank as a fresh canvas. “I... don't remember what happened after that, but I remember grabbing it by its tail and swinging it into the air. Then it felt like- ...like someone else was in control. I remember feeling sore, I think I might have fallen from something. My sister healed me a bit and my mate came to help out but the conjure and its friend were gone by then- I don't even remember killing it, to be honest.”

“I see...” The quiet boy ponders.

“I went inside to get some meds and I started seeing and hearing some freaky lady walking around the house. She had *really* pale and manky, bloody hair. I heard a voice too but I'm not sure it was hers- I don't even know if she's real, I think I'm starting to lose it... She got so close to my face that I could have licked her nose. I panicked and swung something at her but when I blinked there was this little red ribbon on the floor. The bottle was back in its place, and I was stood in a bathroom with nobody else there."

The strange, bewildered boy looks at Kevin in sympathy. "This has all made you very tired, I can see it in your eyes... You wouldn't happen to have picked up the ribbon, would you? I'd like to have a gander."

"Sure-" Kevin replies, rummaging through his jacket pocket. "Here you go. It doesn't look all that special to me though."

Kevin shakily pulls out the deep red ribbon and hands it to the boy who gently takes it with both hands. His youthful face begins to conform to a stern look, concentrating on the ribbons' abnormal proprieties. He holds the ribbon closer to his chest and closes his eyes tucking it between his hands while applying huge amounts of magic to the scarlet silk.

The trees and grass begin to shake gently, dancing in the wind that radiates from the boy. Leaves start to swirl around the two like a tornado as the plants around him begin to glow with a whimsical energy. He calls the promise of the woods to his fingertips and presses into the ribbon's very being. The earth stills- and the mysterious boy returns the ripped silk to Kevin's hands.

"There's definitely something special about it. I say you should hold onto it, like a lucky charm of sorts." The boy smiles.

"What *exactly* did you just do? There was nature magic and then everything started to turn green." Kevin questions.

"I just had a look at it, that's all." He smiles back at the bewildered man.

Somehow, I doubt that... Kevin's inner voice groans.

Kevin doesn't get the *truth* he thinks is being hidden from him- and the boy just smiles, folding up his fishing pole, dropping it into his bag. He throws his sack over his shoulder and bids Kevin adieu.

“This world is filled with many strange and unexplainable things- things mortals just can't understand. When you finally do, come and find me again. Maybe we can share another snack and you can tell me your understanding of the unexplainable.” He turns away from Kevin and holds the strings of his bag tightly.

“Hey wait! I didn't even get your name.” Kevin shouts.

“Oh, my name?” The boy looks back, looking at Kevin as if thinking of one off the top of his head. “...Call me Jay!” He winks at his new friend, who was feeling a lot better now thanks to their chat and shared snacks. Jay readjusts his hat and ruffles his hair when a long, dark antenna-like thing springs out from under the beanie. “Can I have yours?” He asks in response.

“Oh sure, It's Kevin.” He replies, bewildered yet again at the strange appendage he saw under Jay's knitted hat.

“Kevin... A name sharp as a sword and swift as the wind! It suits you well.” He replies as he turns to walk away once more in solitude. “I'll see you soon then, Kevin, may the woodlands treat you well.”

Kevin waves goodbye in fond confusion. *He seems like a nice guy.* He thought to himself. Stares into the lake some more, holding the ribbon in his strong hands, he shakes it up and down, gently inspecting the movement and quality of the silk, just for fun.

“I thought we might find you here- You had us all worried!” He hears his sister's voice just a few feet behind him.

“Why'd you run off in such a hurry? You not feeling up to scratch?” DJ asks him.

Kevin replies, darting between DJ's eye contact and the faded ribbon. “I just come here when I need time to myself is all. I'm good now though.”

DJ fidgets with something in her pocket, a music player or a phone perhaps. “That's fair, man- I'm not judging. Never thought staring at a river could calm ya down though. OH, before I forget, Sam wanted to talk to you about that candle on your head, he said he had some hypothesis or something.”

“Yes, thank you, DJ.” Thome suspires. “Alright then, I'll be blunt with you Kevin. Do you believe in the spirits of this world?”

“Not really,” Replies Kevin. “I know a lot of stories and lore though. Ain't it said that spirits give out HRPs to people who need them the most and stuff?”

“Well, yes, that's how that tale goes. If you know of the tales, then I'm sure you know about their symbolic items known as a 'nimbus.' They're said to be a physical reflection of one's astral powers. For example, a spirit of the sea may have gills, fins or might be a literal fish with mystic, aethereal properties.”

“Alright I get it. But what's your point, Sam?”

“Well, you see-” Thome inhales, puffing up his chest. “Your ring of fire may just be one of these fabled nimbuses! If it truly can't burn things and phases through objects; almost like it's on a spiritual plain of existence, then that could mean you're a real living spirit, Kevin!!"

"What?! You've said some silly crap in the past but now you're REALLY talking from the bin."

"Nonsense!" Thome hoots. "This could be a great revelation- a living breathing spirit in our very own mortal world! I've got to go and research this right away- DJ come with me we have work to do!" Thome calls as he runs off in childlike excitement, holding his bag as he sprints off in exhilaration with Ethos flying at his side.

DJ sighs and shakes her head. "Such a kid... Catch ya later Kev, you too Loo-Loo. Nice meeting ya both!" She then follows Thome at her own pace, equipping her headphones as she bops away to the groove of her music.

"I hate it when people call me Kev..." he groans...

"Don't feel so wet about it- it can't be as bad as being called 'Loo-Loo.' Hehe. ...Y'know, I've missed this place of ours." She speaks. "Remember when granny would sit here with us, and we'd throw little pebbles and sticks in to see who could make the biggest splash?"

"I was just thinking about that when I came earlier." He replies. "Sometimes I come here just so it feels like gran is still here with me... It's nice. Maybe we could make a leaf boat and watch it follow down the water."

"That'd be fun, but there aren't any good leaves this time of year."

"True-" Kevin roots in his pockets and picks up the piece of scarlet ribbon he found in the house. "There's this thing though." He throws the silk into the river and stand promptly.

Leah stands with him and asks. “What're you doing?”

He replies with a kid-like grin “We can't make a boat so we can follow this ribbon instead. Let's go see where it ends up!”

Surely enough- the current of the gentle stream pulls the ribbon in, carrying it along the slow and tranquil waters. The two slowly make chase as the ribbon swirls and dances like a mermaid, spinning and turning elegantly through the stream. They take a walk through the woodlands deeper and further than they have ever before as they pick up hints of a sweet floral scent, magical flowers spread all around their path. Red and white roses, wild orchids and an abundance of hydrangeas covered in popping red flowers.

Leah asks. “You're the one with the greener thumb. Don't hydrangeas change colour depending on the minerals soil?”

“You ain't wrong.” He responds. “It's a bit wacky how they're **all** red though. This dirt here must be pretty balanced.”

The two continue walking down the winding river, admiring the crimson flowers and lush green trees, until it leads into a small damp cave around the hight of a door.

“Ooh, spooky. You wanna go in?” He asks his sister.

“Sure, why not?” Leah retorts. “If there's anything bad in there then you're the one that's battering it, not me.”

They walk into the cave; their first steps emitting a resounding echo as they walk deeper into the bowels of the earth. Leah's hard-heeled boots make most of the noise, clapping against the rough, rocky ground.

“The stream carries on through here.” He notes.

The two walk more, struggling to keep sight of the ribbon in the dark waters. That's when Kevin strikes his foot against the floor and creates a fiery glowing wisp; its flames dancing rhythmically as it lights up its surroundings. Leah and her brother press on with the wisp slowly floats over the ribbon with Kevin's guiding point.

They venture even deeper into the wood's maw until they spot a small but sudden dip in the river, it ends here- into a small spring that flows through a crack too small to crawl or walk through. The fire wisp drops into the water and makes a cat-like hissing sound.

Leah picks the ribbon out of the water with her wand before it gets lost down the small crack in the cave's walls. The only glow now emitting faintly from Kevin's halo; still yet to extinguish. though not very bright at all, it illuminates the walls and floor around them enough.

“Welp... dead end.” Kevin mumbles. “It was fun while it lasted though.”

“It's not over yet, look over there!” Leah points to another dim light in the cave. From where they can see, all that emits is a faint passionate glow around the corner. They peer around and although the light was indeed foreboding- it also felt somehow familiar. A comforting red glow that wrapped its loving embrace around the foliage that decorates the small grove. The light nurtures the plants, loving and caring for them.

The two slowly walk towards the light, Kevin's halo burning brighter; the flames climbing higher with every step closer they take. Just a meter or two away from where the glow came from, both Kevin and Leah can now see the whole opening, the light glistening and flickering like a mini bonfire in the otherwise dark grungy abyss.

Only now that the two are in front of the glow does it thin out, welcoming their gaze through its otherwise harsh hue; both Kevin and Leah stand awestruck. Something amazing and bewildering stood before them partially buried in the dirt.

A single-handed longsword placed firmly in the ground surrounded by the same pink and white orchids from outside, though these stood three times as high, coiling around the sword, yet not touching it. The weapon's hand guard and pummel don a splendid bronze-gold colouring with a faded ribbon wrapped around it in place of leather, seemingly reaching for the torn silk now in Kevin's hand. The blade itself emits a strong red glow akin to a mood light or lava lamp, clearly magical in its craftmanship. Kevin holds out the torn cloth; the glow growing brighter as the torn wrappings around the sword blow towards him, grasping for his robust hand.

He holds out the silk as it flails and flies out of his hand; it joins with the sword in a magnificent display as petals from the orchids spiral around like a hurricane. The ribbon stitches and weaves itself back together seamlessly, taking flight at one end and wrapping firmly around Kevin's arm, fastening itself gently. Then a voice speaks to him, echoing through the cave- but Kevin and Leah couldn't make out the words clear enough.

His halo unfurls into a sparkling trail of embers, colours mirrored. The flames spiral around his body and climb all the way around the ribbon-like tendril that connects Kevin and the majestic blade. The blaze infuses with the wondrous sword- *ZHYUM- FLHOOSH* The blade itself retreats into the crescent shaped hilt with a crackling flash as it slings into Kevin's left hand, not even a centimetre from missing.

The ribbon disappears into a golden light in a coiling way, illuminating the cave. Now holding the sword of his own free will, he peers into its ruby reflection; he sees a woman of echos long sung; curly hair and a silken dress, flowing and dancing like pure water. She holds the same sword that he now holds himself- the one he recognises from the dream.

The words spoken to him just mere moments ago now made sense, for she speaks once more... "It has been a long while since our spirits had last crossed paths... It is so lovely to see thee again... Rah."

Chapter 4
A New Companion

A few uneventful weeks had passed since they found the mysterious blade and October has just begun. The cozy time for trees to shed their foliage to feed the ground for the harsh winter months.

Kevin and Leah made a nice full hot chocolate to sit outside with, enjoying the soft early autumn breeze during sunset in the back garden, with a new *strange* addition. Kevin holds out the hilt of the blade that he and Leah found on their little reminiscent adventure, looking at it closely and feeling the exquisite build.

"So how is it that you can talk anyway, sword?" Kevin asks the sword, bluntly.

The sword replies with a well-spoken, feminine delivery. "One hath always been fluent in speech, Rah. Doth this come as a shock to thee?"

Kevin replies "Who's Rah? You keep calling me that and I don't know who that is. And we don't have talking things in this world, the closest things we have are conjures but those are living things. Also, you've been stuck to me for weeks. Why is it when I put you down, you zipline back onto my wrist with magic ribbons? You're far from normal, swords don't do *any* of the things that you do."

The blade replies- its voice still one-note. "One apologises if mine-own companionship is seen as a doting nuisance to thee. One's intention is to keep thou safe, Rah."

“There you go again, calling me Rah- I'm not a dinosaur, I'm Kevin.”

“Thou barest the exalted flaming nimbus of the sun spirit, Rah. Thy physical form hast undergone many changes over the centuries- yet inside thy memories endure deep within, and thou art still the spirit of the Sun.”

This kind of talk and bickering had been happening since Kevin brought the sword home- against his will at that. He stands up with a groan of discontent slipping between his lips. Leah turns to ask. “Where are you heading to at this hour?”

Kevin replies. “I'm gonna take a trip to the market to see if I can get rid of this magic sentient smart speaker.”

Leah responds in shock. Not much, but enough to widen her eyes. “But you just got her- she's gotta be important to you somehow, she did whatever it was with your halo to make it disappear. I think this is a dumb idea.”

“Look, I'm willing to keep a talking sword but not one that has an answer for everything I say and constantly misnames me among the MANY other things it does that pisses me off. It's going and that's final.”

Leah sighs. “Alright... Just don't get into trouble, okay?”

Kevin gives his sister a single downwards nod. He jumps the fence and launches off towards the town at what he considers a relaxed pace, running down the autumn green fields, watching the trees and grass fly by as he soars on through.

The sword begins to nag Kevin once more. the frustrating part to him being her monotone voice, sounding almost robotic... “Doth thou truly plan to sell mine own vessel on a common market at dusk? Thou can clearly see thy sun setting on the horizon."

He chuckles as he speeds up, now pacing at a brisk 50mph. "Oh don't worry pal, I'll find someone who'll want you alright."

"The chances of thee parting with oneself are 0.001%, this sum being rounded to the closest-"

"Oh my god. Shut up I don't care."

The two argue for what seems like eons until they finally arrive at Lalstrun farmers market, a place where anybody from anywhere can sell their produce, trinkets or old things. When Leah has made enough enchanted jewellery, she brings them here to sell on one of the smaller stalls. Someday she gets lots of customers, other times, not so many; such is the way of selling handmade goods.

Kevin walks around the market with the sword in hand. There aren't many stalls open at this hour- all the farmers who sell their produce have called it a day so they can preserve what hadn't been sold.

Even at dusk, the market has a serene vibe to it, the colourful striped canopies neatly rolled up; the ones still out gently blowing in the evening breeze. In a nearby field, Kevin sees some people training their conjures in a sparring match. It's hard for him to make out the figures but the spectacle is one to behold, even from afar.

The sword breaks his silence. "Did thou not come here to conduct business with the locals, Rah?" the sword asks, almost like its mocking him in a way.

"Oh silly, silly me. How could I forget when you're **tied to my arm like that."** He replies, gritting his teeth.

Kevin begins asking an elderly shopkeeper that he knows well enough if he'd be willing to trade. “Hi walt! You having a good evening? I was wondering if you'd be up for a trade?” Kevin asks with a big feign grin slapped straight onto his face.

The old man replies, tidying up various wands, weapons and cases of mana quartz into the boot of his car. “I reckon I'm having a good'n, sonny. What've ye brought me then, lad?”

“Well-” Kevin shows the weapon vender his arm, entwined with rose red ribbons. “You're into funky weapons, right? I've got this thing- it's supposed to be a sword. Well, it had a blade when I picked it up and then it went *shyoom* back into the hilt- it's got a yap on it too. IF you can get it off my arm you can have it.”

Walt stares at Kevin with a raised eyebrow in utter confusion. “A yap? what're ye talkin' about, sonny boy?”

“It talks and it doesn't stop. It keeps back-sassing me and it's been doing it for weeks!” Exclaims Kevin, tugging viciously at the ribbons that tie the blade in place. “It *loves* Leah, they talk about all kinds of things but when it's me all I get is stupid stuff like, '*Your current probability for success is nya nya nya.'*

The man looks at Kevin, his concern begins to stir as more familiar shopkeepers around the quiet marketplace come forth to witness the strange conversation.

“Go on, then.” Kevin barks at the seemingly useless piece of metal and cloth. “You gonna demonstrate your lip or what?” Yet the sword does not speak... Not a single sound comes from the magical weapon.

“OOOOOH, no I get it. You only like talking when it's convenient for you? Fine then.” He shouts and wails at the dormant sword. He swings the dead hilt up and down intensely, trying to get it to behave and speak... Yet it still speaks not.

The market sellers stand around him, all looking at him as if they were watching a screwball lunatic fight his own shadow. At this point Kevin had enough, he knew what he was going to do.

He was going to return the cursed sword back to where he found it in the first place. Bolting from the farmers market and dashed all the way back to the village, he flits straight past his house and through Flogging Woods, running down the river once more as he's beaten by the gnarly branches along the way.

He scrambles between the thick tree branches and through the red foliage that trails over the path to the caves mouth; the same place where he and his sister threw the silk into the river. However, this same cave no longer stands where it once gawked.

Completely puzzled by this, he asks. “Sword... Where's the cave?” He asks, staring sharply at the quiet tool in his hand. The sword speaks not, and he asks again. “Sword, where, is, the, cave?” And just like the last time it yields little response. Kevin grumbles and densely grips the hilt of the blade; he flings the confounded thing at the rocks with an astonishing heave which leaves an impressive hole in the terrain; falling to pieces as the rocks crumble around the sword.

He sits quietly as the evening light gently tucks itself away on the horizon, turning twilight blue in its captivating hue. He looks at the river, which still flows directly through the hill, just without the cave to accompany it.

A cave doesn't just ***disappear,*** *does it?* Is what he asks himself, peering into the river again all alone. And just like clockwork the sword bursts free from the rubble and slinks around his arm once more.

Kevin bows his head. "...Why do you keep following me?" He asks, deadpan, pulling the skin of his face down.

The sword gives him the exact same response it's been giving him for the past weeks. "One is here to protect thee, this is something thou should hast claimed awareness of by this time, Rah."

"Yeah, I know that I just- You- WHY are you protecting me? If you haven't noticed- I don't need your help, I live a pretty peaceful life and you're completely throwing off my-"

The Sword interrupts him abruptly. Suddenly it coils down his arm and into his hand. Its hilt crackles with energy, entering its blade form. "Silence thyself, danger looms near."

"Don't tell me to shut up I'm trying to be reasonable with you-"

It interrupts once more. "Continue this foolish bellowing and thy risk of death shall increase by 57%."

Kevin snaps back. "Oh, never mind my shouting, what about the GIANT RED GLOWSTICK IN MY HAND!?"

Suddenly, a group of hooded felons numbered three fly out of the foliage with barbed black sickles, swinging for Kevin, drawing deathly close to his neck; a hairs-width away from slashing his windpipe and ending his life. Yet out of the blue, the vein sword takes charge of his body-changing colours from a crystalline red to a dark blood-crimson. The sentient sword lifts Kevin's arm against his consciousness and slices the hooded foes forearm clean off, cauterizing the wound instantly before a drop of blood was spilled.

The veiled lady screams as if hell itself had entered her body. Staring at her arm on the floor then quickly looking back at the stained sword, he wails. "HOLY SHIT WHAT WAS THAT!?" He shouts.

The sword warns him again, ignoring his frantic state. "Stay on thy guard, one cannot take control of thy clumsy arm another time ere long. Focus."

Kevin grips the mystical short sword properly yet with the most unfitting posture one could use. He stands tall with his legs not secured to the ground at all, leaving him completely open. The other two hooded figures circle him; their weapons raised above their faces with low guards.

The sword raises its voice, still robotic and stiff yet far more stringent. "Stand properly, the object of thy life exists at risk! Doth thee even fathom how to wield a blade?"

Kevin flips the sword around in his hand, creating rings of red light as he does so. He stares the foes down barbarously and smirks. "...You'll see."

He disperses with a loud thundering crash. The two crooks almost sent flying off their feet as the third lurks on the ground, writhing in pain and seething through her teeth. They prowl around and peer through their hoods, searching for their target in the twilight... The trees around them rattle and rustle as they hear a distant resounding crash. Then another; the trees dance again. And again, the sound grows closer and closer with each wave of their leaves. A scarlet red glow forthwith makes its way into view; bouncing from tree to tree.

Kevin emerges like lightning from the sky and slashes from behind, immobilizing one of the remaining shrouded men. The nimbus of Rah ignites over his head; he lands and spins with the wind of a hurricane, hucking a massive amber curveball of fire straight into the last enemy's chest, knocking them off their feet, burning a hole through their mantal. The shrouded crooks take their time struggling in pain to raise themselves up.

They look not at Kevin but at the floor in bitter shame as the sword commands. "The foe is down- this battle rests in your favour, finish them post-haste!"

But Kevin stands undaunted, leering at the assassins. He kicks dirt at them with a peck at the ground to gather their attention. "Now piss off. The next time I see you I'll do more than cut off an arm." And at his mercy the three dishonourable felons leap and stumble away with ninja-like speed, taking the severed arm with them...

Kevin and the sword watch them clumsily trip and flee from the scene. The blade asks him, "Why did thee not deal the finishing blow? Such mercy leaves an unclearable stain upon the honour of a fighter."

He responds simply. "Just because they were trying to kill me, doesn't mean they deserve to die themselves."

The befuddled sword deactivates its blade. "Thy logic confuses me greatly. Thy style of battle displays the intent to deal lethal blows, yet thou decide to show mercy. One must ask again, why?"

But Kevin dismissively replies as he begins walking along the trail. "I don't think it matters too much, does it?"

The crimson blade speaks. "If thou hast any true issues then mine ear is thine own, if thee wish to share your burdens."

"Thou wishes not." Kevin responds with sarcasm.

"Then thou hast not any obligation to do so..." The sword replies, solemnly.

"Actually... I do have one problem..." He adds.

"Prithee, let thy voice be heard. What vexes thee?"

"You keep calling me Rah. I don't know if you've gathered by now, but I hate it. You keep telling me all these probabilities and other useless things that I don't need to know. You just forced your way into my life and you're not even paying attention to how I feel about your input."

The sword grows solemn once more; as the sun begins to set, the two watch as the horizon cycles through its shades of nightly blues. "Doth the exalted title truly upset thou to such a strong degree?" The blade asks him.

"Yeah..."

"Doth thee, with all honestly remember not a single memory of our times once shared?"

"Nope."

After thinking about it for a long minute, the sword speaks once more, and Kevin feels a warm sensation in his hand. “So be it, then...” The sword continues. “It is clear to oneself now that Rah does not share the same fortune as oneself... She hast been gone for a long age, as such, one shan't use her title to address thee any longer. From this moment fourth, I shall address thee by thy given name, Kevin. Is this more to thy liking?”

“Hey, you're starting to catch on, sword!” Kevin booms loudly.

“Then allow oneself to express the joy in knowing one can title thee as such. One apologises for the upset one hast caused thee...”

“Hey, it's water off a duck's back now. No use sweating over it.”

And with that, both Kevin and the sword had learned to respect one another a little bit more. Although he still found her quite annoying, the two were slowly growing fond of one another.

Kevin lets a smile slip before asking the sword a question. “Yo, sword. You can see stuff, right?”

“Indeed. One can see the world beyond this vessel. Is there a reason behind thy asking?”

“Just wait, I wanna show you something.” He responds as he begins to jog through the dimly lit woods.

Kevin takes his time getting to his destination, yet the talking sword doesn't mind the slow-paced walk. In fact, one could go as far enough as to say it seems to enjoy the slower paced side of Kevin.

They pass through the canopy of trees quietly, seeing the night-time critters come out to hunt and play. The owls of the night begin to hoo and stalk the land for their prey whilst the hedgehogs and mice scurry around the mats of fallen leaves, scavenging for their breakfast.

Kevin had been jogging for a while now, but finally the two come out of Flogging Woods and are welcomed by the rocky hills of Lalstrun.

"There is an abundance of beautiful landscapes in this small village of Lalstrun." The blade speaks.

"Yeah, I know, right? Sometimes when I'm bored, I use my God-Speed to go hill jumping. I don't really have anyone else who can do it with me though 'cause no one can keep up."

"One is unfamiliar with these terms 'hill jumping' and 'God-Speed.'" The blade puzzles.

Kevin looks at the sword fastened to his arm. "Oh, uh... God-Speed is what I called my HRP."

"One must apologise for asking thou another question. Whatever doth thee insinuate by 'HRP?'"

"HRP just means Hyper-Real Power. You know how some people have rare magic mutations? That's what that's called." Explained Kevin.

"One now understands." The sword responds. "May one ask thee a final question?"

"Go for it."

"What is 'hill jumping?'"

Kevin stumbles again. Even though the explanation is easy and on the label, he still struggles to explain. "Well, it's like- well it's kinda hard to explain to someone who's never seen it before. You ever heard of pinball?"

"'Pinball?' Thee leave me more flummoxed than before this elucidation began..."

Kevin presses his heels into the dirt. "Instead of trying to *elucidate* why don't I just show you!? Hold on tight!"

Bounds from the ground; the ribbon of the sword clings to his arm with the force of a strongman's grip. He shakes the land and spooks the woodland critters into their hiding spots, landing atop the closest hill they were stood before. "You ready, sword?" He asks with a huge grin on his face.

"What should one be preparing for!?" Her calm exterior now shaken by Kevin's illogical and brash bound.

Kevin presses down once more; the world grows quiet. Nothing but the sound of the wind atop the tall hills of Lalstrun blows through their ears... Then he rockets off with a booming shockwave, leaving a crater in the hillside, redirecting the very wind-flow itself as it carries him along to the next hill, then the next, and the next! All the while squealing with glee as he flies through the air like a hawk.

"See!?" He yells over the force of the wind. "Isn't this fun!?"

The hilt blinks red in rapid succession as the voice within begins to fill with hysteria. "KEVIN! SLOW THY PACE- CEASE THIS FOOLISHNESS. THY RISK OF INJURY IS ASTRONOMICAL, L-LAND SAFELY AT ONCE!"

“Come on, lighten up a bit Scarlet, enjoy yourself!!” He responds whilst completely blanking her demands.

“DO NOT IGNORE MINE OWN ORDERS- LAND THIS INSTANT!”

“Ha-ha, see it's not so fun being ignored, is it? We still have a few more to go, hold on!”

Even though Scarlet didn't like it very much, deep down she found the experience quite thrilling- soaring through the sky with Kevin as the sun took its final moments of the day to watch. And somewhere even further deep down- It reminded her of someone close to her... Kevin lands safely, just as she requested; his hair windswept and frazzled.

“**That's** what hill jumping is. What do you think?” Kevin asks with a childish grin.

The sword whispers. “Thou...”

“Yeah? Thou *what?”*

“Thou called one Scarlet.”

“What? I've gotta call you something don't I?” He questions. “What do you think?”

“...It brings my heart great joy. One shall cherish the gift of this name, Kevin.”

He giggles. “Weird way of saying ‘thanks’, isn't it? You speak like you're from the 1600s or something. Let's try working on that, yeah?”

“...My apologies.” Scarlet speaks. “One thanks thee. Is this better?”

“Missing the point, a little Scarlet- but you're getting there!!”

“One is glad. One now believes it is a good time to go home now. Shall we depart?”

“Mach-1 or 2!?”

“A leisurely pace is more than enoOOOUUGH-!”

Kevin blasted off with a grin still stuck on his face and Scarlet screaming against the wind. The two probably hadn't noticed it yet but they had already begun to form something special- a friendship that would be difficult to break and one that would shift the tides of what was yet to come...

Chapter 5

Interlude: Bothersome News

Meanwhile, in a land where the yonder is painted a dashing jade green; where silent mountains of snow cradle a palace of lilac and blinding white, sat a very irked king...

“Sire,” Three shrill voices whale down the blindingly pale halls. “Sire, we have returned from our mission!” They shout from beyond the tall doors that separate them.

The king stood busy in his echoing, pristine throne room, admiring the artwork on the walls as he silently polishes a mahogany display case and an astounding gathering of mythic ornaments with his court jester attendant. After making sure not a speck of dust remains, he places an expensive looking, ivory vase back into the cabinet, locking the magically sealed glass doors.

He turns to the door to hear it knock once more. “Let them in, will you? This had better be **very** important- I'm in the middle of my pre-holiday seasonal inspection...”

With a big heave, his attendant yanks the tall wooden doors with a strong heave and steps to the side, the few guards and conjures present all bow their heads as three mercurals; one female, the others male, run into the room and drop to their knees, giving blessing to their exalted and benevolent king, clad in lilac with hints of maroon and mustard yellow.

The man on the left unveils his face, speaking out of breath, coughing and gasping for air as the sweat soaks his hair. "Y-you grace us with your- *hack* with your light, my great- *cough* lord."

The king unempathetically turns his back to the struggling man, walks up to his throne which rests atop an unnecessarily tall twenty marble stairs. Each second step he takes the man below him chokes and splutters more. The monarch sits on his velvet cushioned throne and speaks, his voice only being amplified by the long, tall hall. His voice breathy, suave and proper.

"Do finish choking before you open your mouth before me. I trust the three of you have a report that will put me in a good mood before I depart for my *much-needed* vacation?"

"My lord!" The second man speaks, removing his black hood also. "I humbly request your forgiveness on Shade's behalf, he's sustained an injury and has had little time to rest since our return."

The King answers with silence. He stares them down from on high in complete quietude. The woman then speaks next, all three servants now exposing the tops of their heads as they bow in exalt; the light shining through the mighty stained-glass windows. "My lord, I too have sustained injury..." She cries under her breath, holding her elbow tightly.

".........And you, Murk?" The king asks, with his thin elbow firmly placed into the armrest of the chair, his gaunt face pressed into his pale fist.

"I am mostly unharmed, my lord. At most I've experienced minor burns, however I am still in fit working condition."

The king still sits in uneasy quiet; a grim wind hits the room. The beach-skinned monarch breaks the deathly silence. "Do go on..."

"Y-your highness." The writhing woman speaks up. "Our target was trickier than the three of us could manage together; our ambush was unsuccessful. However, we've gained valuable intel from our encounter. Your suspicions were correct, my lord. We can confirm that the spirit of the great star... has returned in a new form."

"..."

"..."

"..."

"What?"

The three speak in ghostly unison. "The Great Star, the Guardian of the Deserts, the Spirit of the Sun, has made their return, your greatness."

The king abruptly stands from his throne, his skeletal arms shaking and his ghostly eyes twitching. Sparks of magic on the sides of his head form a pair of decorated horns; butterflies and elegant lining carved within. His godly white eyes glow with an inhumanly fierce gaze. His beautiful, poise face had twisted into a wicked scowl.

Walking down the stairs slowly, the sound of his heels tapping on the marble filled the room with a feeling of dread. One step at a time, the feeling grew more intense in the cores of his subordinates. "Say that again." He demands, the light in the room fading away as the artwork on the glass turns to grey.

"S-sire?" The man named Shade gasps for air. He and his comrades all raise their gaze.

Panes of glass in the darkening, chilling hall begin to crack and shatter through the power and white rage that suddenly boiled over within him. "SAY THAT AGAIN." He roars.

The three knelt paralyzed in fear, failing to utter the words that the king demanded them to repeat. He stands at the bottom of the stairs, still looming over their incompetence with malice.

"You mean to tell me, that an ordinary HUMAN overpowered three of the best assassins in all Silvalon, and the only spoil you return to your master with is worthless information that I already knew...... Is that right?"

"My liege- He's simply not normal!" The woman wails in defence. "His sword commanded him to finish us all off, but he spared us- Our lives flashed before our eyes."

The room had fogged and became chilling in its aura, the guardsman and the king's jester all began to quiver at the cold. His white eyes shine like twin lanterns in the gloomy, foggy twilight. He lifts his arm towards his three subordinates, and a sneer stretches across his dimly lit face. "...Then let me fix that for you."

Three whistling sounds shoot through the air, a purple light cleaves through the mortal barrier as if it were a hot knife through butter... Three corpses now lay in the pale marble throne room. He slowly walks towards the three husks that lay in the centre of the room with a raised hand.

A flair of indigo magic from each body raises upwards and towards his raised arm, entering his palm. Shaking off the sensation, he raises it once again with a flaming blue aura, walking down the straight carpet as he whisks his arm to the left; all three carcasses follow his direction, flying across the hall like discarded ragdolls.

"Clean this up by the time I'm back from Belivana..." The baleful king adds.

"On it! Is there anything else, milord?" His unsettlingly happy jester asks.

"On the day of my return in two weeks, I expect the seasonal ball to be fully prepared. In addition, I expect the guest list to be prepared too, and do not dare to forget the V.I.P. guests. Are we clear, dear jester?"

"Crystal, Sire! I'll inform you as soon as the duchess has finished getting ready so you can leave at your earliest."

"Splendid. It's delightful to know that I have at-least one competent peon in this palace.

Chapter 6
The Try-outs

A few days later, Kevin was back at work again. For today's afternoon lessons he had joined with Thome. The two tutors shared a double period in wind magic casting- something the great Multi Mage excels at. Most of the lesson on Kevin's end consisted of him hanging back and watching due to his lack of expertise in this element.

Even though the interruptions last time were inconvenient, students throughout the college watched the mages of the house fight off conjures until it was safe to return home and learned a lot just from spectating.

Today, there was a lot of student gossip spoken about those fights; Kevin being the focal point. As it would be expected, the Grand Mistress Christine had caught wind of the chatter. At the end of the day when all the students had left for home time, Kevin, Thome and Scarlet enjoyed a moment of respite. The three sat happily in quiet with only the sounds of pen on paper and Kevin rocking back and forth on his chair.

“Thou are going to fall.” Says Scarlet to Kevin, mixing the old English she fondly uses with a more modern vocabulary, one word at a time.

“I'll have you know I have impeccable balance, Scarlet.” Replies Kevin.

“So does the chair when it's on four legs.” Thome butts in. “I have papers to mark and you're distracting me with your creaking and squeaking.”

“Fine, party pooper...” Kevin replies defeatedly, holding himself still on the chairs two hind legs.

Scarlet replies to Thome. “In Kevin's defence, thou might find it ideal to invest in two dozen stone stools, as they sit cold and silent, unlike thy wooden chairs.”

“Who asked you?!” Thome bickers back.

“Twas a kind suggestion on my master's part.” Replied Scarlet- monotone. “Might one also make note that the six previous documents you have penned contain grammar mistakes of your own work.”

Thome furiously stutters back. “What- Who- Just be quiet, you! You should know that the pen is mightier than the sword.”

Kevin starts to rock on his chair again, forced by habit. He adds. “It is if the wielder can spell properly.”

Thome lay verbally slain by Scarlet's sharp words. He wrote his papers in silence, eyeing her with an annoyed look every time he wrote a word longer than six letters. He marks his final paper, dotting his pen triumphantly, taking a sigh of relief- “So, I noticed your halo has vanished. Good for you.” Thome utters to Kevin.

Kevin Replies. “It came back a few times, but it only seems to do it when I’m angry or when I use heavy magic. I don’t really understand it all that well. Scarlet did some ribbony thing when I found her and then it just went *nyooom* and disappeared, just like that.”

Thome replies. “So, your sword-”

Scarlet quickly corrects him once again. “My name is Scarlet.”

"So, ***Scarlet*** must have some connection to the spirits then." Thome finishes.

Kevin sits up. "What gives you that idea?"

"Think about it for a moment," Thome begins to ramble. "Isn't it peculiar that along with making your halo go away- She survived a throw from your HRP? Only a spirit is beefy enough to take that kind of damage."

Kevin thinks about this for a while, until Scarlet slinks down his arm and levitates before the two of them, a holographic red screen bordered by silk ejects from the crescent hand guard and shows a diagram, along with an explanation. "Allow one to enlighten thee. Kevin bares the exalted nimbus of the Sun Spirit, Rah. This is an indisputable fact. However, when a spirits life meets its tragic end, their astral soul is recycled as they leave behind a rare trinket called a Spirit Stone; though perilous to destroy, a spirit's being is recycled anew if broken."

"So, what you're saying is that I'm just a dead Egyptian lady stuffed in a mid-twenties English guy's body?" Asks Kevin, rhetorically.

Out of nowhere, the glass door of Thome's classroom swings open for the Grand Mistress herself. The sudden shock of her appearance throws Kevin's *impeccable balance* off, landing him on the floor. "You'll be a double dead lady if you don't explain all the gossip that I've been hearing about you!"

Shocked by the sudden interruption, Kevin falls back from his chair. Scarlet projects a scoff. "One thought you bore impeccable balance."

"I did until I got jump scared..." Kevin replies. "Hi Christine. What's this about rumours?"

Christine puffs up her chest and throws her curly locks behind her shoulder. "I have heard none-stop chitter chatter about the return of this sun spirit in all my classes for days now and it's all been focused on you, Kevin. Explain."

Kevin relays the past events to the best of his ability, omitting some irrelevant details to make his explanation swifter. "So, in a nutshell, I have a sick new talking sword, and I'm apparently a spirit reincarnated or something."

"And I assume this *Scarlet* is your new weapon?" Christine asks.

"The pleasure of meeting thee today is all mine, Grand Mistress." Replies Scarlet, taking an invisible curtsey.

"Well, well! Someone knows their manners! It's a pleasure to meet you too, dear~"

Christine and Scarlet get acquainted with one another. Scarlet then goes into a more detailed explanation of Kevin's nimbus, recounting as much information of Rah's crown as she can- though her memory stood a bit rusty.

"I see..." Christine mumbles, "So, Kevin could be an ancient spirit reborn. This does open a new can of worms for you both, not to mention the conjure portals for the college."

Kevin responds. "Can we all stop talking about me and comparing me to some dead Egyptian lady? Making me feel insignificant right now..."

"Sorry Kevvy, dear~ I didn't mean to hurt your feelings." Says Christine. "I have a suggestion for you though. The Advance Heroes are having try-outs at their headquarters in Rowanshire tonight. Sammy, you should go too! You can apply for a senior magic officer's licence, just like mine."

Kevin's eyes sparkled with childlike excitement at the single mention of the Advance Heroes; a group of skilled mages and fighters who work to protect the peace of the world. Their roster is packed with HRP wielders and skilled fighters, and most importantly- his hero, Zapp Susanna.

Kevin tunes up his excitement to eleven. "You really mean we can go and meet Zapp Susanna!? Like, right now!?"

Christine replies, peeved. "Of-course not right now, did you not hear me? You have a whole three hours to go until the try-outs begin. And you're not going to run off before Thome, you two are going together whether you like taking the train or not!"

Kevin replies. "Can I not just run and drag Sam with me?"

Thome replies with a peeved look on his face. "Don't be stupid. Ethos and I aren't being beaten and pulled along just so you can worship your little washed up super-hero."

"Hey, she ain't washed up-" Kevin bites back. "She's got far better lightning powers than you, that's for true!"

Thome stands, angered. "Oh yeah!?"

Kevin and Thome bicker and shout amongst themselves. At the side of their squabble, Scarlet speaks kindly. "Grand Mistress, may one inquire as to what these try-outs may hold? More information on what to expect may very well increase chances of acceptance into the Advance Heroes' ranks."

"Well, Scarlet dear. The try-outs are held twice a year for fighters of exceptional skill; a mere apprentice would be turned down at the door just from the very sight of them, you also need a magic officer's licence to be accepted in~ As for the try-outs themselves, you'll be sparring against one of the Advance heroes greatest. Whoever you fight will also be one of the judges who decides if your application gets reviewed any further."

Kevin speaks, breaking from his argument with Thome, excitedly. "So, all I gotta do is kick someone around and I get to join!? HA! Keep up Sam, I'll meet you at the train station!"

With that, Kevin swings the door open and revs up his power, before something quite peculiar catches his eye. He stops as soon as he sees what looks like a sealed letter. He picks the envelope up which dons a pressed texture and a lilac-coloured wax seal with a butterfly stamped into it.

Kevin turns to Christine and Thome. "Huh... There's a letter here..."

Christine raises an eyebrow. "Who would come up to the top floor to deliver a letter? Honestly- that's what our front office is for."

Thome asks curiously. "What does it say, Kevin?"

"I don't know-" Kevin groans. "It's not bloody opening. I think its magically sealed or something."

"Prithee, allow me." Scarlet asks of Kevin to hand over the letter. Holding it up, he aims Scarlet at it. Her sparkles with a dazzling magenta and ruby red light, firing her blade as a thin laser that shatters the seal on the letter like ice.

Scarlet then shifts into a small letter opener form. He opens the letter from the side and a sudden burst of bright light shines out of the envelope, causing Kevin to drop it on the floor; a sheet of paper comes flying out like a firework. it floats into the classroom and lands gracefully on the table with the other papers.

"Wow... Okay then." Kevin sighs, bewildered.

Thome picks up the paper, yet there seems to be naught on it. He turns it over and just like the other side- not a single trace of ink, print or anything useful on it. "Did someone seriously go through all that trouble just to send a magically sealed letter with nothing on it?" He fumes.

"HI THERE!!!"

"AAAH!" Thome screams, jumping up and hiding behind Christine like a frightened child. Ethos leaps before the suddenly talking letter, growling as her aura spikes and ripples.

The paper had sprung to life out of nowhere. A split tore perfectly down the middle to make a pair of legs, and a face quickly scribbled on like an invisible pen was drawing it. "Sorry if I scared you there, friends. My names Note! Specifically, Note number eleven of one hundred! It's my esteemed pleasure today to deliver a message of GREAT importance to two wonderful people in this room! Kevin Marrowald, Grand Mistress Christine Adamson, it is my duty to deliver a very special invitation to you both today!"

“Woah, slow down there Christmas card- I have so many questions.” Kevin interrupts. “There's A HUNDERED of you!? Who's your master? What-”

The Note interrupts Kevin back. “I'm terribly sorry, Kevin but I'm afraid I'm on a tight scheduled and I won't be able to answer any of your burning questions today. My master is very strict y’see, so my metaphorical hands are tied.”

She continues. “Master, the esteemed, exalted, benevolent King of Blanc has invited the two of you to the seasonal autumn ball of Blanc, held once every season at the Pale Palace on Ivory Crown Peak to commemorate the great legends and higher ups of Silvalon! You two however, are considered some of the few guests of honour and have been chosen for other means, which my kind and benevolent master will discuss with you upon your arrival!”

“H-hold on a moment!” Thome shouts. “Why does *HE* get to be the one to go to this esteemed ball? *I'm* the legend here- all his feats are just lucky happenstance. I've broken bones and lost blood to get where I am today! How is this fair!?”

Note #11 crumples up a bit “I-I'm horrendously sorry sir, I didn't make the guest list. I'm sure that whatever it is you do, you do the best out of everyone...”

Thome grabs his bag and storms off with mard; Ethos in tow, leaving the door wide open.

“Wait! What about the try-outs?” Kevin shouts down the hall.

“I don't need to be lectured on my worth by a talking piece of toilet paper. Go by yourself!” Thome shouts back.

The thin conjure from the envelope looks distressed, guilty even, her face scribbles again as a sadder expression draws in- her eyes furrowing. “Oh dear, did I say something wrong?”

Christine inhales as if she was about to reply, but Kevin speaks over her and explains bluntly. “No, you didn't say anything, he's just a massive tetchy mardarse. You can carry on.”

“Thank you, the only thing you two need to do now is sign the papers here in the envelope and bring them with you to the World Gate to the northeast of Carvina! The exact meeting place is on the address, along with all your other information!!”

“Hold on a moment.” says Christine, softly. “There’s an old Silvalon World Gate in this very town? This is news to me I'll tell you.”

“Of course, there is. They're all over the planet! It's just been repaired from waaaaaaaay back; master says you can't fully destroy a World Gate’s connection. Anyway, I must be going now, I have a few more invitations to give out before my job is done. Thankyou both for your time and I hope I see you at the ball!”

The small conjure, no bigger than a tissue proceeds to jump into the air and glides through the classroom window, leaving the fancy envelope behind. How did it even get in there and who left it? Christine reads the letter in her head, the contents include the exact same things that Note said, with an additional date and time of when to be at the World Gate, along with a map of where to find it.

Kevin looks at the letter too. “I'm probably gonna loose this, can I leave it here and get it on the day?”

Christine replies “No Kevin, the day of the ball is on a Saturday. The college would be closed on that day dear~”

“Oh, right.” Replies Kevin.

Scarlet speaks. “Prithee, Grand Mistress. Would you be so kind as to take Kevin’s invitation into your care?”

“Of course, Scarlet dear. Well now, let's not dawdle any longer, shall we? Let's get to those try-outs! Getting there early might mean you have a fighting chance at going first!” Sings Christine.

So, with a burning goal fresh in mind, Kevin, Christine and Scarlet in hand all set off to the train station, even though Kevin would have been more than happy to run the whole way whilst giving Christine a piggyback.

The G.M. locks up all the doors for the night after a wearisome day. They board the train which already lay in waiting at the stop. Reading the timetables, it takes about half an hour to get to Rowanshire from Carvina, and Kevin isn't too impressed with the time it's taking at all.

“Can trains not go faster?” He asks, kicking his legs back and forth like an impatient child.

Scarlet responds, “Should my equations hold true, at the velocity we are traveling, I believe we shall reach Rowanshire in approximately twenty minutes from now.”

“Twenty? That's so long thooouuughh...” He whimpers. “Can I not just jump off at the next one and run? I can get us signed in before 5:30.”

“No, Kevvy dear. You need to learn to relax and do things by the book for a change.” Says the Grand Mistress. “After all, this is one of the faster trains on this track, It's an Azurian Bullet! Built and imported all the way from Azure in Silvalon!”

“Silvalon- that's where the gates go too right? Really dumb question incoming: how come there have been mercurals living on earth all this time even though the world gates are just being fixed?” Asks Kevin.

Scarlet answers his question. “Silvalon, the domain of mercurals, and Earth, the home of humans both coexist as parallel planes of existence. In the times past, those travel points served as connections between the two planes. Unfortunately, one holds no information that led to the destruction of the gates. In consequence, mercurals who were left behind were forced to settle down permanently after the connection's severance. Try as they might, it proved impossible to call every mercural back to their home world.”

Christine replies. “My eldest boy adores his history; I remember him telling me about how the war of Blood and Mercury ceased after the World Gate’s destruction? Perhaps that's why they were all shut down; to stop all the fighting.”

“Your hypothesis is likely to be the truth, Grand Mistress. One wishes to ascertain its accuracy for thee; however, mine own memories are... inadequate.” Replies Scarlet, her glowing voice growing quiet.

Kevin asks her a question, trying to lighten the mood. “Hey, Scarlet. You said you've been around for centuries, right? I'm guessing you had another owner at one point. Do you wanna talk about them- what was he like?”

“My former master was not a man,” She speaks fondly. “Illuminating the circumstances would prove challenging to someone who lacks context of my history. In simpler terms, one may claim that my previous wielder was none other than myself.”

“Wait, what? How can you be your own wielder AND weapon at the same time?” Kevin asks, bluntly.

“A considerably long tale mine is; a tale stretching across centuries of valour and sorrow. It is unfortunate that our short train ride does not hold the needed time to speak of my past.”

“You're that old, huh? So, if you used to be your own wielder does that mean you had a real body at some point?”

“Real?”

“I didn't mean it like that-”

"Hehe, ‘twas a jest, Kevin. I understood what you implied.”

Kevin sighs a breath of relief, “Hey- you just laughed!”

“One is amused you found amusement in my jest. Though let us return to our previous discussion. One indeed bore a form before my confinement to this vessel; I was once a being of metal and magic, a Mercural.”

Christine leans forward in her seat. “You mean to tell us you once had a true form all those years ago? I'm sorry if it’s rude to ask of you dear, but how long ago was it before you were turned into a sword?”

Scarlet replies. “That would depend on the current year, Grand Mistress.”

“The year is 2014, dear~”

“O- oh...” Suddenly, Scarlet's voice quietens even more like a massive weight tied to her ankle had just been thrown off a cliff, dragging her down with it.

“Well, how long ago was it?” Kevin asks, holding the sword tightly. Unable to think of a way to comfort her.

“If my memories are correct, then four hundred and twenty-four winters have passed... It is likely that my allies and comrades of yore have long since departed from this life.”

Kevin sighs. “Scarlet...”

“One senses your sympathy and appreciated your care, and though it is not necessary, I thank you regardless. One had accepted this long before our first meeting in the realm of slumber, though hearing this from you only reaffirms my haunting suspicions.”

“Well, you've got me if that's worth anything.”

“It is worth more than thy weight in gold, Kevin.” Scarlet replies with a tear dripping from her metaphorical eye.

Though her era had ended many years ago, it made her ecstatic that she could still find new friends in a time where everything feels upside-down to her. The lightning-fast train finally comes to a smooth halt. Many people exit the train from their daily commute to school and work, Including some pupils from the college.

Christine and Kevin take their step off the platform; a place rarely visited by them fills their eyes. Carefully tended trees and shrubs on every street corner that fill the town with a lush, calm aura. A welcome sight for stressed and weary eyes; flowers filling hanging baskets on the train platform. There are even wild geraniums and cornflowers growing on the trainlines, and the faint but sweet smell of nectar fills the air.

“So where too, boss?” Kevin asks.

“Let's see. It's been a while since I've been to this little garden town. I don't have my mobile phone with me right now, so I can't search for a map. Do you have yours, dear?” Asks Christine in return.

“Not on me, no. I leave it at home on a workday.”

Scarlet replies. “One does not understand the capabilities of this ‘mobile phone’ device well enough to help in this regard. However, if all that is needed is a simple map, I may be of assistance. Prithee, Kevin, hold my vessel skyward.”

Kevin holds his arm up high as Scarlet's ribbons climb his arm and around his hand. The blade points skyward, humming as it glistens and shines in the afternoon sky. A single stroke of light slides down the blade, once it hits the hilt it disappears like usual in a sparkling flash.

“Mapping is complete!” Exclaims Scarlet. “One now has access to a three-mile diameter map of Rowanshire, with the centre point being where we now stand. With this information, providing directions to the Advance Heroes main headquarters should prove trivial. Please proceed off the train platform and leave through the closest exit.”

“That's so cool!” Says Kevin, excitedly. “How does that work exactly? Is it like echolocation or something?”

“Please proceed off the train platform and leave through the closest exit.”

"-Ok."

Kevin and Christine follow Scarlet's directions to the best of their abilities, though her wording sometimes needing clarification. Her words got so messy that sometimes they missed a turn and had to turn around. Eventually, Scarlet began to use simpler instructions like "Please turn at the second left." "Please use the crossing before you." And so on. Kevin and Christine walk and talk whilst the crimson blade concentrates on giving accurate directions.

Kevin asks. "Why did Sam go off in a strop like that earlier? He's a fully grown man but he kicks off like a kid when nobody pays attention to him."

Christine replies. "Kevin, dear. Do you remember the time when Thome went off to learn magic back in Spain where his dad lives?"

"Yeah, we were good mates when we were kids. He left without saying much; didn't even keep in contact, so I just kind of, y'know, stopped bothering."

"Samuel moved to Spain with his father to attend the academy of magic in Aldea Esmeralda. In his own words, he wanted to prove he could be 'just as good as you.' You're a very strong man, Kevin- far stronger than he could ever hope to be. Just thinking about that throws him into a fit, and I believe when that Note conjure told he wasn't invited to a ball specifically held for exceptional people, that just about did it for him."

"Was all that really because he thinks he's not as good as me? He's got a lot going for him though- he's way better than me by a long shot, he's mastered every element of magic. No other human on the planet has that kind of power."

“The feeling of inferiority is a powerful enemy, Kevvy dear. One day, you might be in Samuel's boots for a change~”

Kevin tries to sympathise with Thome in his head, failing to understand how someone could feel like that when they have a sole unique quality themselves. He would have gladly given the invitation to him if he’d thought of it at the time, but now it's a bit too late for that.

After more directions, turning streets left and right under the amber streetlamps, the group arrives at the Advance Heroes headquarters. A grand old chapel standing tall, bandaged by the modern structures and plating that holds the decrepit building together with banners flying high. Its clock tower ticks away with the flag of the Advance Heroes flying high on its mast; a depiction of a simple black crescent moon.

“What happens now?” Kevin asks Christine.

“Well, we go in and register for the try-outs~” Replies Christine as she turns, curling her hair around her finger. As the Grand Mistress turns, a young woman sprinting as if running for her life suddenly crashes into her. Headbutting Christine, she drops several folders, all with a big red sticker on them. Both ladies fall down onto the cold flags. Scarlet sparks energy from her hilt and swings towards Kevin's hand, though Kevin pushes her away as he bends down to lend Christine a hand.

“Oh my...” Christine wobbles back on her feet. “Why are you in such a hurry, young lady? You're lucky I'm a tough old girl or you could have really hurt me.”

“D-Désolée- Sorry Madame, I'm in a big hurry-” The strange red-haired lady stammers. “It won't happen again, I promise!”

“Good, I should hope not.”

The quick though albeit awkward endeavour ends abruptly as the woman scoops up the papers she dropped and carries on running for the hills. Why would somebody be carrying something like that in their jacket?

Kevin looks at Scarlet, fastened to his arm. “And what the hell do you think you’re doing- you could have got us both in seriously deep shit, Scarlet. You don’t just go into battle mode unprovoked.”

Scarlet explains, “One sensed an 11.4% increase in the chance of conflict.”

“That's not a big enough increase for you to risk us getting turned in to the Advance Heroes right outside their own home base. If there was an uncontrolled monster or something running around, then that's a different story.”

“Then allow one to apologise, Kevin. One's intention was to protect you, not for you to be apprehended by the authorities. One shall inform you that this vessel is not solely built for harm, as I have the capacity to restrain my strength and enter a middling state which only pacifies opponents. One knows all too well how fragile humans can be.”

“Alright, but when we get home, we’re setting some ground rules for that.”

“Well,” Christine adds. “I'm less concerned about who's hurt and more about those files she was carrying.”

“Bet she stole them.” Kevin adds.

“That hypothesis came to one's mind also.” Says Scarlet, calmly.

Kevin strides on. “Aaaaanyway- we came to put me in the try-outs so instead of threating over something that doesn’t concern us, we should get going before applications close.”

“Agreed, let us make haste.” Scarlet replies.

Kevin, Christine and Scarlet walk through the gates of the gargantuan building- hailed by beautiful rowan trees, rose bushes and lavender shrubs. Small waterfalls and manmade streams run through the courtyard with carefully crafted bridges arching over them. Decorative fish swim around the deep, clear waters that flow before the old chapel. The old clock tower is affixed to a building that wears a more modern appetence- clearly built centuries apart. Yet surprisingly, the old brickwork doesn't clash with the modern panel and glass-based structure. A strange synergic mix of eras coexist on the outside of the chapel.

Our group walks through an automatic door, stepping into a clean white tiled room with several front desks and a very busy waiting room packed with people- there are several conjures sitting with their masters. Kevin spots several small ones sat on their master's laps, nestled in their pockets and perched on their heads; small recognisable creatures like birds, mammal-based creatures- and some more abstract creatures too.

One in particular catches Christine's gaze- a stunning electric creature borne of a mix between organic and mechanical with a mane of fan blades; its body and limbs completely incorporeal. Its tail of three long braided wires, swaying and swishing as the beast makes fair purring noises as its master strokes its fur.

“Hello sir and madam, how can I help you today?” A tall mercural lady approaches Kevin and Christine.

Kevin focuses his attention. “Hi. I'm here for the try-outs.”

“Of course, sir. You've arrived at a good time! And how about you, madam, will you be partaking as well?” The staff member asks Christine.

“Oh no, dear~” Replies Christine, musically. “I'm much too old to be testing my metal with these young ones. I'll just be spectating if that's alright.”

The kind lady responds. “Of course, that's wonderful. Now then sir, please follow me to my desk and I'll have you all signed up and ready. First, I'll need to see your magic licence.”

Kevin rummages through his jacket pockets and pulls out his wallet. He takes out a plastic ID card with his full name, date of birth, and magic authority level...

“Ah, there appears to be a problem with your ID, Mr. Marrowald.” The lady notes.

“What? What's the problem?” He replies, uneasy.

“It says here that your use of magic has been under oversight since the last five years.”

“Wait, so I can't join in because of that? How is that fair?”

“Unfortunately, due to the level of oversight placed on your licence, you’re restricted from using destruction and manipulation magic unless you're on duty at your workplace, or in self-defence. As this is technically a sporting event, I can't permit you to join. I'm very sorry."

Kevin scoffs. Defeated, he simply swipes his ID and walks away. Christine begins to talk with the lady at the desk, seemingly frustrated with the annoying though reasonable rule. Scarlet kindly asks Kevin to wait for Christine to finish talking before going leaving. Although his urge to just go home festers strong, Kevin heeds her advice and sits down in the waiting room with the other people.

He grows fidgety, bouncing his knee rapidly, not realising just how fast he's doing it; wearing down the rug and shaking the bench which causes people and their companions to move. As he carries on rumbling the bench and floor, a muscular, eye-catching woman walks in, accompanied by a shorter- unremarkable man.

The first is a tall imposing woman with a thunderous aura about her, raising her voice to a much shorter man with hair as white as snow who wears a knitted scarf and warm coat despite it being quite warm outside; their conversation seemed more like an argument to Kevin. Suddenly, his brain sparks, noticing the dark shaved hairdo, the yellow faired dress and her black mechanical boots- his eyes widen as the Storm Commander herself makes her presence known.

Kevin's eyes practically sparkle with admiration- wishing to go straight up to his hero and introduce himself eagerly- yet the crowded halls prevent him from doing that. With all the other background noise going on Kevin and Scarlet found it hard to understand what she was shouting about. The yelling finally stops as she looks around the waiting room, eyeing up everybody up, though to Kevin's dismay- he doesn't even get a glance.

"H-hello, everyone..." The unremarkable man speaks softly. "Can I have your attention please?" He calls with barely any power behind his sheepish voice; quiet as a mouse. "Hello? A-anyone...?" Still, nobody hears him over their own noise.

The tall lady stomps on the floor, the hydraulics in her boots crash against the floor with the sound like that of a shotgun blast. "EVERYONE SHUD'UP AND LISTEN." She roars. With a dramatic shift in tones, she exhales and speaks to her companion, gently. "Go on Frost, you've got the floor." She gently pushes him forward. With the room now quiet, he speaks again.

"H-hi everyone, my name is Henry Wolfarth and I'm the Frost-Borne hero, l-leader of the Advance Heroes... I'd like to say- I, uhm, t-thank you all for coming today. The uh, turnout is a lot better than last year's try-outs. Um, now if it's okay, I'll let my college here explain everything..."

The tall lady puts her hand on his shoulder and steps forward. She speaks with that same loud, commanding voice. "Alright, the names Zapp- Storm Commander; second in command here. Listen up cause I's only gonna say it once. You'll all be competin' against our houses strongest to see if you've got what it takes to be in our ranks; brute force alone'll get you hurt here. You'll be paired VIA random selection and go in ascendin' order; each fight'll be one on one. Conjures are forbidden and weapons'll be enchanted with a bluntin' effect for the duration. Anyone who ain't feelin' up to snuff should withdraw before the try-outs start. Y'all's got five minutes before startin' time."

The quiet man, Henry, speaks up again. "T-thankyou, Susan. Now then everyone, l-lets draw the lots for who you'll be squaring off against. Please all que at desk number three."

The dozens of mages, warriors and aspirers all line up cordially at the desk, one by one drawing lots to see which hero they'll be sparring with. Kevin on the other hand still waits for Christine who had been rudely pushed out of the queue. Amidst the line of people, Christine sits down with him and places her arm around his shoulder, giving a squeezy hug and her deepest empathy to him alone.

"I'm sorry, dear. I couldn't do anything to change her mind. I know how much this meant to you..."

Kevin replies, holding back a tear; trapping his emotions. "It's fine. It's not like it's your fault. Just wish I didn't have to have my licence under stupid restrictions..."

"Kevin," Scarlet alerts, "Could you explain to oneself what it means to have your magic licence under oversight? If now is not a good time, I shall ask again later."

"You're only going to keep asking if I don't tell you..." Kevin grumbles. "A long time ago I was teaching a magic lesson that went tits-up. Since then, I've not been allowed to use it in public spaces, only my workplace or home."

"Does this restriction count for all five categories?"

"I can use summoning, enchantment and support magic but not manipulation or destruction- *unless* it's for self-defence or work."

"And what of your Hyper-Real Power?"

“That's part of me, they can't exactly chop off my legs, can they.” He responds humorously.

The line had shortened, and the people had been moved outside rather quickly into the training grounds with their companions. With only a few people left, Kevin stands up and walks towards the main exit. *No point in staying to watch if it's only gonna make me feel crap.* He thought to himself. Scarlet remains quiet as they follow.

“Uhm... Excuse me.” A gentle voice calls out to the trio as they were just about to leave. They turn around to see Henry, holding his scarf tightly for comfort. “A-Are you not going to draw your lots?”

Christine explains the situation for Kevin quickly, getting Henry up to speed on what had happened. Still holding his scarf, he thinks about what to do for a moment, fiddling around with his hands anxiously. He Kevin to follow. He sits behind one of the other desks and uses the console; he shakily asks to see Kevin's licence again. Although he doubts that'd do any good, he still hands it over.

“Oh, I-I see the problem you mentioned.” Henry whispers, quietly. “Half a decade of oversight restrictions... Just give me a moment- l-let's see if I can't do anything about it.”

Our group waits for Henry whilst he apprehensively taps away on the monitor. The large foyer grew quieter, the amber of the evenings settling in fast as the rays of sun that shone through the windows faded away.

The line by now had completely disappeared and the only other people left were themselves and the single receptionist. Henry hands Kevin a ticket with his name on it, the number nine and the name ‘Susanna Bol.’ Kevin only needed to see the first few letters of her name before he started jumping for joy.

"I-Is there something wrong?" Asks Henry with a concerned look as he anxiously rises from the computer.

Although Kevin doesn't reply, he holds the ticket like an excited child with the biggest grin known to man on his face.

Christine replies heartily, "You should take that as an 'everything's good,' dear."

"Oh, r-right. Well, everything's starting in the back, so you should follow me." Speaks the Frost-Borne Hero.

"Wait a sec-" Kevin interrupts. "Took a while for it to sink in but... I'm in, just like that?"

Henry stutters, "Well, uhm, more or less. I'm the manager so I can just kinda *do that.* And you came all the way from Lalstrun, so I didn't think it was fair to send you away because of some small technicality."

"How'd you know I was from Lalstrun?" Kevin asks, putting Henry on the spot.

"E-Everybody with a H-Hyper-Real Power is on the Advance Heroes system. I-It doesn't mean you've done anything bad, it's just a legal thing we need to do... that's all..."

In spite of the ominousness of what Henry just said, a sense of relief finally washes over the trio. Now following Henry, Kevin and Christine walk with him to the rear courtyard where several staff members await with the warriors and mages of the house.

Zapp Susanna stands in the centre of an open circular arena with several machines surrounding it. The ground within being white sand, surrounded by two outer rings, one with shallow flowing water and the other baring very common looking shrubs.

People in Rowanshire sure love their plants. Kevin thinks to himself.

It is an architectural tradition in Rowanshire, Kevin. It has been so since one was a child. Scarlet's voice whispers in his head.

Surprisingly unalarmed, Kevin answers back in an annoyed tone. *Is that you Scarlet? Why am I not surprised you can pry into my thoughts, how long have you been doing that for?*

Since we have been united. She replies.

That's really creepy- why've you've only just started to talk back now?

One did not wish for my telepathic abilities to become a nuisance to your everyday life.

You're already a nuisance. Just don't do that unless you need too, I like to keep my thoughts to myself.

Zapp creates a crackling ball of pure yellow power no bigger than a ping pong ball. It twitches and sparks sporadically with electrifying energy, flicking her hand up, shooting the magic into the air, it pops several times to call everyone's attention. "Alright, the first fight's startin' in less than two minutes. All spectators have gotta stay three meters away from the arena. And like I said before- NO conjures allowed. If you summon one of any kind you're disqualifies. Fighter number one, step forward- your fightin' me."

The first contestant steps forward, A muscular mercural man with a shaved head, donning typical body-building clothes. The man punches his fists together as he enters the ring, summoning two golden gauntlets clad in spikes; seemingly being born from metal magic.

Zapp turns, offering her hand to the opponent in good sportsmanship, but the man swats her arm away with aggression.

"I gotta fight this overblown legendary hero? Are there no REAL warriors here?!" He gloats in a generic brutish way.

Zapp grumbles and snaps her fingers. Without saying a word, the staff members understand exactly what she wants. Loading the projectors with mana quartz, the barrier emerges from the machines that surround the arena. Holding the shrubs, waters and sandy ring in its glossy glowing bubble

"You sure you're ready for this, old man? I don't want you crying to the uppers if I break your back." Zapp asks the beefy bald man.

"You don't look so tough, little girl. I' betcha I can squash you like a mouse between my fingers!" The bull replies.

"Fine whatever, let's get this over with..."

Zapp raises her arm skyward as the clouds start to churn, she holds her head high, her short hair standing on end- her lips begin to speak. "In my heart, a storm brews. Embracing it, I empower the commander within!" She flicks her hand around and a wicked white thunderbolt crashes down into her hand, forming a pole in a split second. She strikes it against the floor and sparks the end of it into her signature axe 'Ms. Thunderclap,' jittering with the power of storms; it shimmers and charges the air around it.

Kevin stares at the axe of raging storms and shakes in glee as he tries to contain his excitement- his feelings exploding inside as he finally gets to see his inspiration fight in real life.

"Alright then, tough guy. Let's rumble." Zapp roars, instantly storm dashing to the giant of a man as she hurls her axe over her head, striking the man with a flash of dazzling power. She drops low as the man stumbles, blocking the blow with his gauntlets. As she crouches low, she flips onto her back and jabs the man in the stomach with her black hydraulic boots- a powerful jolt from her heel punctures through the air and roars straight into his gut; two hits are all it took to take the man down...

"Lightning strikes down the arrogant. People like you don't belong in our ranks. Someone get this poor fool out of my ring..." Zapp scoffs, spitting on the ground next to him.

The barriers lower and the man is carried out of the arena by his legs by two men.

"Oh my. That was brutal. I'm sure glad I didn't sign up with you, Kevvy dear." Christine spoke, her hand trembling.

"So cool......" Kevin murmurs, his mind completely gone at the dazzling performance that stole his eyes.

The referee calls out the next fight, and the next, and then the next, and then the next after that; the first five contestants all went down without much trouble at all.

But as a surprise to everyone, the sixth fighter, a short girl who knocked and shot her arrows with incredible precision managed to fell the Storm Commander in thirty seconds with shots so fast they were rendered invisible. Zapp appeared shocked to say the least. Rising from her hands and knees, brushing herself off, she gives the girl a firm, silent, but very proud handshake.

“It isn't easy to beat Zapp like that in a fight.” Said Christine. “She's a very powerful opponent. Most people who get put up against her don't ever get chance to land a single blow. I hope you know what you’re getting into dear.”

Kevin’s face practically radiates admiration to the point he starts to drool at the mouth, as if his brain had completely shut off. “Super strong....... Gonna win......”

Scarlet speaks. “Reclaim your senses, Kevin. ...Kevin?”

“Don't worry about him, Scarlet my girl. He’ll snap out of it once his idol takes a well-deserved breather." Sings Christine.

After six fights, the last one ending up in her defeat, Zapp sits the next one out to rest. Kevin snaps out of his trance-like state, just as Christine said he would. At this point new fighter must take her place, but who? A new person steps up, and to Christine’s humble surprise, it's the Frost-Borne Hero, Henry.

“You're up, Frost. Make me proud, bruv.” Susanna speaks, patting him on the back.

Henry whispers. “I-I don't think this is- ...What if I-”

Zapp interrupts him. “Hey, just focus on keepin’ your cool. You've got this, K?”

“I-I’ll try. Uh, contestant seven, d-due to the Storm Commander being unable to continue, I'll be t-taking her place. Please step up to the arena.” Henry speaks, anxiously.

A young man with red hair walks into the arena, no older than seventeen. He shakes Henry's hand and walks to the other side of the arena. The Frost-Borne Hero mumbles something under his breath and takes off his heavy looking coat, doing some light stretches before placing his hands together. Striking his knuckles, he slowly pulls them apart to draw a set of glistening blue iridescent icicle claws.

“What's he mumbling, Scarlet?” Kevin asks, curiously.

“One is uncertain. He seems to be under emotional distress.” She responds, concerned in voice.

“Can't you read his mind to find out what’s shaken him?”

“Unfortunately not. One can only read the mind of ones I am under the embrace of. My telepathic powers are limited to a short duration. One used this gift to protect you from those hooded felons in the woodlands. One sensed the urgency in your heart and struck in your stead.”

The referee sends the signal, and the red-haired boy strikes first. He spins the sand below him around his arms and blasts it at Henry in huge gushes. Though the blizzard stood firm and unmoving- his scarf blowing in the breeze. The sand blades grew lethally close to him before he scratched his foot against the floor and lifted his arm skyward, creating a wall of glistening blue and lilac crystal ice.

The crowd cheers and hoots for more before Henry leaps above the peak of the ice like a kangaroo and dives down like a kingfisher, slashing the ground deeply with his claws.

Kevin calls out to his bladed companion in his mind. *I'm confused, Scarlet.*

She responds with haste. *What bewilders you?*

I've watched every broadcast of these try-outs, even the ones held before I was born, and I've ***never*** *seen this guy before. Plus, he's using an element I don't even think Sam knows.*

Perhaps Henry and yourself are not so different in constitution...

What's that supposed to mean?

Scarlet did not answer Kevin's question, secretive and vague as usual. The battle continued still, both combatants holding their own- yet the sand wielding challenger grew tired and sluggish; his movements led uncoordinated. Even though the challenger grew weak, Henry's reserves of energy were still full to bursting.

"I guess it's time..." Henry speaks from behind his blizzard of silent gusto. With one swipe of his claws, the challenger fell to the floor; he had lost, yet the crowd still cheered for both for him and the victor. Without time for a rest, Henry glares down at the audience with red bloodshot eyes, his breaths long and sharp demands the eighth challenger to step up. His breathing sounded heavy, and his posture looked tense.

“Something seems different about that young chap-” Christine comments. “That skittish man from before has completely disappeared. I smell trouble afoot...”

“He does seem more aggro than before...” Kevin adds.

“Shall we incapacitate him when our time to battle arrives?” Asks the Scarlet Blade.

“I’m fighting Zapp, though.” He replies, stubbornly.

The next fight began quicker than expected, and it was swifter than the last by a huge margin; about ten seconds before the challenger fell unconscious. Henry's breath grew heavier, and his eyes grew with an insatiable lust for battle. The magical barrier started to form condensation from the sudden temperature drop within.

The mages of the house take down the barrier to replace the mana quartz before resummoning it. Henry glares at Kevin with the eyes of an apex predator- sending a frozen river of shock down his spine.

“Get up here.” Henry points his claws at Kevin. “I want to see what that Hyper-Real Power of yours can do!” He barks down.

Swallowing down his anxiety, Kevin flips Scarlet into his hand and her crystalline blade forms in a spectacular flash, as ever. Kevin passes through the hole in the barrier as it closes behind him. “I'm supposed to be fighting Zapp, though.” Whimpers Kevin, glaring at her name on his ticket.

"So what?" Henry Cackles. "It's far more fun fighting someone who's just as savage as yourself!"

"Hold on a sec snow boy-I've been called a lot of things, but savage? I prefer to not smack people around if the option's available."

"That's not what your records said- COME ON, LETS START ALREADY!"

The referee gives the signal; Henry races towards Kevin, slashing his frosted claws at him with the fury of a bear. Kevin skips around the arena, dodging Henry's slashes and batting the occasional close shave away with Scarlet- all the while building momentum gradually.

"I can turn a blind eye to you calling me savage, but taking my fight slot up crosses the line." Says Kevin, hopping back as he continues to dodge the wild slashes of his opponent.

"And what happens when that line is crossed, Marrowald? HUH!? You can't dodge forever- You're gonna have to hit me back sooner or later!" Henry screams.

For every swing he takes, he seems to lose a drop of that timidness he displayed bare moments ago. His personality has completely shifted from introvert to a ferocious caitiff. The arena had grown significantly colder than before, and the arena bubble had practically become opaque; Kevin could practically see his breath.

"Kevin-" Scarlet calls. "You cannot deflect his blows forever; he is gaining the edge."

"Hold on- I've got somethin' brewing." Kevin replies. With his built-up momentum he flings himself from the barrier and over Henry's head, using the speed he'd built up to sling a giant crimson energy blade from Scarlet. The blazing projectile crashes down; Henry tanks the attack with a jagged wall of Ice, scowling at Kevin from below.

“I'VE GOT YOU NOW!” Screams the Frost-Borne Hero as he shatters the ice wall and hurls each glistening shard at Kevin in a mystical gust of hail. Kevin falls to the ground wailing, dust and snow cloud up the arena. Kevin had been hit by nearly every single projectile.

“Oh my...” Christine spoke, worriedly. Out of the two she would have expected Kevin to be the clear victor, but now doubt fills her heart; she's not so sure anymore. The referee circles the arena to try and see Kevin's condition through the frosty condensation before calling the match. But unexpectedly, a shimmer breaks through the snowy fog; a flickering glow of amber. A ring of fire emerges from the clouds and the dome becomes clear once more- donning the nimbus of Rah, Kevin stands firm.

Henry pauses, it's the only break he's taken since he began, mesmerised by the familiar flickering glow of Kevin's halo. He chuckles under his scarf, which quickly turns into a sinister cackle like that of a witch. Kevin fully emerges, his eyes burning white hot. His clothes wear new tatters and Scarlet's blade reflects one the shine of the dome in the evening light; a dark bloody crimson colour.

“See-” Henry whales. “Exhilarating isn't it!? This is the most fun I've had in AGES!”

Kevin replies bitterly. “You’re mad... You’re beginning to piss me off big time, frosty.”

“That's enough, Henry!” Zapp Susanna shouts from her bench. “Get down and cool off already-”

Henry turns around screeching down at her like a banshee, his face contorting and bending like rubber at his unsatiable rage. “SHUT YOUR TRAP, WOMAN. I'M NOT FINISHED WITH HIM YET-”

The spectators concerned looks grew wider and daunting. Though before the cold-hearted man could even turn to face the sun spirit, he finds himself on the receiving end of one of Kevin's mighty kicks. A laser-fast triple roundhouse at blinding speeds- shattering the barrier of sound and magic like glass, launching Henry to the other side of the courtyard; the people stood in disbelief.

The barrier goes under emergency shut down from the dramatic malfunction and Henry crashes into the wall, paralyzed by the pain as the brickwork crumbles. He peels off the brick wall and flops down to the ground unconscious; blood trickling from multiple places on his head and back. His icy aura blowing away completely upon the impact.

Susanna calls out to him, franticly rushing to his aid. Christine soon follows, galloping with healing magic swirling mystically around her arms. The barrier is lowered as more people go to check if the Frost-Borne Hero is okay.

“You overdid it...” Scarlet shuns Kevin.

“You TOLD ME to do that- what do you mean!?” He argues back.

“Striking an opponent when his back is turned... Unchivalrous.”

Kevin reluctantly leaps over to see if Henry is okay, holding himself in pain. He pushes through the thick crowd and crouches down next to the injured, bloodied man. The evil look in Henry's eyes had vanished and all that remained was the soft man from before, unconscious and barely breathing.

“Is he okay? I didn't mean to-” Kevin is interrupted.

“Is he okay?” Susanna barks. “DOES HE LOOK OKAY? If I weren't still beat right now, I'd rip off your-”

Christine intervenes. “Please, both of you settle down. Let the poor man rest.” She speaks as she holds a heavy earthy magic over Henry's bleeding head.

“Is there anything I can do to help?” Asks Kevin.

“No...” Susanna responds. “You've done enough.”

Scarlet speaks to Kevin, telepathically. *One believes you are no longer welcome here. One thinks it would be best if you departed promptly.*

Kevin swallows his shame and walks away. No speed, no swagger or power in his step, only shame and disappointment in himself. Thinking his chances are now squat, he slumps away, though he and Scarlet can't help but wonder why he was so aggressive. How can someone so soft and unthreatening turn into something like that, and how is someone like **that** the boss of the entire Advance Heroes organisation?

Thoughts and feelings overwhelmed his mind at this moment- a lot has happened in such a short time. Kevin sits outside the Advance Heroes offices and checks his phone. If it hadn't somehow been cracked before then today was its unlucky day as the top left corner was completely shattered and caved in with cracks running through the screen like spider-webs, making it barely visible. He tries to swipe up, but it responds not. Aiming to pelt the phone against the floor furiously, Scarlet quickly snatches it from his hand; a beam of scarlet-red light flows from the hilt and catches it before he has a chance to bounce it off the pavement; absorbing it magically.

“Harbor no anger towards your valuables as they cannot think or feel- nor is your mobile phone responsible for what has just transpired.” Scarlet speaks in a calming, authoritative way.

“I know that, I'm just pissed off- I can't get anything right! Every time I want to do something big it always blows up in my face and I get in shit. Ever since I became a teacher, I've had the worst luck. It's not fair, Scarlet- I just wanna get ONE thing right... just one thing...” He whimpers, sorrowfully holding his face in his hands.

“......Kevin, you are still young. At each moment in life there will be hapless events that stem from one's own misdeeds. This happens to all living creatures big and small and there is naught one can do to transpose events that have already happened. Though whether it be your own fault or another's, there shall always be opportunities to right those wrongdoings.”

“You-” Kevin sighs a breath of relinquishment... “Why are you so good at speeches? It ain’t fair...”

“A speech should come from one's heart... I too have made errors in my time. And for every action I have erred in, I shall help you avoid and correct one of your own.”

“Thanks... Can I have my phone back? If it's still working, then I wanna talk to Leah.”

"It is damaged beyond use, Kevin. One can deduce this from merely holding it. However, providing It remains in my care I may be able to use a power of old to restore its main functions."

"Yeah? So, you can fix it?"

"Not at this moment I would need similar materials to reconstruct the devices components, and a source of great power. I can however intergrade your phones functions into this vessel, until that time comes."

"Thats cool, you're a sword of many talents! Can you give Leah a bell now?"

"A 'Bell?'"

"I mean call her, please."

Scarlet projects a neon holographic screen with cracked edges and shards levitating around it, creating a magical display of the uncanny blend of ancient and modern technology. The screen held the bare minimum information: a hang up button, a volume slider and Leah's phone number on it- which is still incredibly impressive for a sword and a broken phone in his opinion.

"Yo Lee, can you hear me?" Kevin talks through Scarlet.

"Yeah, I can hear you, is everything okay? You're pretty late home today." She replies.

"I went to the try-outs in Rowanshire and broke my phone, but Scarlet ate it and now I can call through her."

"That's a *peculiar* way of saying it. Anyway, I'm just glad you're alright. Sam told me all about the try-outs anyway. How'd it go?"

"...Bad."

“Oh no, did you get hurt? Is there a magic pharmacy nearby?”

“Nah I’ll live. I'm sore but I'm not hurt-hurt.”

Scarlet interrupts abruptly. “Your brother was in direct collision with forty-eight projectiles of an unknown element. He is lucky he can still move.”

“WHAT!?” Leah screams; the call audio crackling. “Kevin that's serious! what would I do if I lost you, huh!? I'd have no family left at all...!”

“I'm sorry, okay- I don't like making you worry. You're always patching me up and running around after me. It's not fair on you...”

“That's part of being your sister, you twit. How bad is it? Be honest.”

He sighs, unable to hide the truth, “I've got cuts everywhere and my skin feels like it's on fire. My phone is smashed, and my favourite jacket is in shreds.”

“Kevin, I want you back home right now- I don't give a monkeys arse about what you say- I don't want you getting into any more trouble.” Leah shouts, her voice shrieking and breaking up over the connection.

“Leah I'm fine. I'm just a bit beat up- I'll live.”

Scarlet interrupts. “One is in personal agreement with your sister, Kevin. You are in no physical condition that warrants you to not return home and rest.”

Kevin answers back, bitingly. “Did I ask you?”

Leah replies. “Kevin she's right. You need to come home before you hurt yourself again. Your power might make you tough, but it only protects you from yourself. You're just as vulnerable as the next person... Just come home, please.

"... Fine, I'll be home in an hour." Kevin sighs as he hangs up. The holo-screen disappears and scarlet weaves herself back onto his arm.

"One has remembered the current position of the sun and shall remind you in sixty minutes time." Says Scarlet.

"Well, can you not?" Snaps Kevin. "I know how long an hour is, I'll be home by then."

Completely ignoring her master's request, Scarlet asks. "Would you be requiring directions home, or are you to ride the train?"

"Don't start with the mapping again- I'll find my own way. We're taking a *quiet* walk first..."

Kevin and Scarlet depart at an unhurried pace as he takes his time to clear his mind, admiring the sleeping flora and trees of the streets of Rowanshire; walking solemnly in the amber sunsets gaze as the old timey streetlamps turn on.

A breeze blows by as Kevin peers down from a canal bridge to see the barges and boats all berthed by the edge- as the soft wind blows by the sweet scent of flora wafts into his nose. He stays here for a good twenty minutes or so, a third of his time to get home is up. Scarlet kindly informs him of this, but he remains silent- lost in his own mind, just letting the gentle breeze carry the scent of autumn flowers to him.

"Do you smell that?" Kevin asks.

“Which scent are you referring too?” Scarlet asks in response.

“That sweet, medicinal smell. It comes from those chrysanthemums over there. They smell a little bit like menthol.”

“One cannot lie; one can no longer smell the subtleties of scents I was once able to... apologies.”

“It's fine, I just wanted to share that with you. Was my gran’s favourite, it was.”

Scarlet pauses for a moment after that, before asking Kevin a question. “Your gardens at home; is it you who tends to them?”

“It's a bit of both of us, even Mobbee helps out sometimes. We picked a lot of it up from our gran. The garden's not as good as it was when she was around, but we try our best.”

“You and Leah speak of your grandmother fondly, were the three of you close?”

“Yeah, we did everything together. She took us to school, cooked our meals and put us to sleep at night. We used to sit in front of the fireplace and drink hot chocolate in the winter. We still do that sometimes... it makes us feel like she's with us.”

“There was once a time when one sat around a fireplace with her kin too. We would sit in the gallery of the sacred grounds during cold winter nights, drinking whisky and ale. On celebratory occasions, one would tell fables of valour and legend to the townsfolk as my comrades would sing and dance along. It would be dishonest if one told you that one didn't long for those days...”

“Sacred grounds? Sounds like you had some friends in high places, Scarlet.”

“One means not to bluster; though the ‘one in the high place’ was my own self.”

“No kidding? Was you a house lady or a duchess or something?”

“Set your sights a little higher, Kevin.” Scarlet giggles with a digitized echo.

“Are we talking royalty!? Get out! Sounds like you had a sweet life.” He raises his voice in disbelief.

“Twas a very privileged position, though one mourns not for benefits of the crown. One spent her days making taking care of my kingdoms people, providing clothing- food and clean water to poorer folk in need. Twas onerous work that often left oneself depleted- though the satisfaction of seeing the smiles of those folks was like none other. Alas, that roll in one's life had come to an end centuries ago.”

“You still do that, though.”

“One does what?”

“You still make sure everyone is okay, even though it's Mobbee, Leah and me. You remind me to eat, shower, check the news, clean the dishes. And you always tell me that my heartrate is too high and when I need to calm down- and yeeeaaah, sometimes it’s annoying, but you're only looking out for us... I appreciate that.”

“...You have my sincerest gratitude for your compliments. They touch my heart deeply.”

“And there you go with your big appreciation speeches again. Out of all your speeches those are *definitely* the most awkward.” Kevin chuckles.

“He-he, one could call this habit carried down from my own era.” Scarlet chuckles in tandem.

The two enjoy their modest conversation. Reminiscing about the foregone past had brought an understanding to Kevin; which put him in a bit of a better mood.

Bringing Kevin out of his shell a bit helped Scarlet wiggle out of her own; even if only a little bit. From the distance, some rather loud sounds could be heard. Though it's hard to make out, they hear the sounds of shouting and banging.

“Did you hear that sound, Kevin?” Scarlet asks her master.

“I think the try-outs are still going on. Choosing to ignore.” He responds, bluntly.

“Your choice as likely as not, is for the best.”

“So, like-” Kevin thinks for a moment. "Back in your day, were you a princess, queen or something completely different?”

“One took the title of-”

The loud indistinguishable noises startle the pair again, Kevin becomes increasingly frustrated as the echoing waves interrupt their conversation.

Biting his tongue, he asks. “OK that doesn’t sound like its coming from behind us. Seriously, what is that?”

“One is unsure. Perhaps a street scuffle has flared up.” Scarlet responds.

“Whatever let's go home. It ain't our problem anymore.”

“Indeed, let us depart.”

Kevin picks up speed and stumbles down the road in the direction which the sounds were coming from, having no other choice as his footsteps crackle through the air. Scarlet notifies Kevin.

“Kevin, you are currently approaching the origin of those unsettling sounds. I advise you to take a longer route for the sake of your own wellbeing.”

“I wanna get home as quick as possible-”

“You claimed not ten seconds ago that it was not of your concern. Why must you always be so incomprehensibly stubborn when one instructs you!?”

“Maybe I wanna be nosey and have a quick peak.”

Scarlet scoffs for the first time ever at Kevin’s stubbornness. They arrive not a moment too soon to see the origins of the commotion. A fight had indeed broken out outside a mana quartz distribution factory. At this time the factory should have shut its doors for the day, however- a lady stood firm, clutching her leather jacket tightly; squaring off against a group of five in trench coats and similar leather jackets.

“You have placed your nose where it does not belong; you have seen the source of the uproar, now let us leave.” Scarlet says, hurrying Kevin to move along.

“Hold your horses, isn't that the lady who we saw running off with those paper-file things?”

“The probabilities are high; her features are identical to the maiden earlier encountered. One must be inclined to agree.”

As the onlooking man and his talking sword gaze from an unnoticeable spot, the woman seems to be getting defensive as she reaches inside her jacket for something concealed... The coat wearing challengers approach her with what seems to be elementally charged firearms, glowing at the tip with multiple colours of light. In tow, they carry blunt weapons on their backs. Kevin's hands begin to twitch in anticipation.

“Do not intervene Kevin, they all bare weapons. your chances of becoming fatally injured will be of galactic proportions should you engage.” Warns Scarlet. “Be wise and leave this scene before you too are dragged into the conflict. You may be faster than sound, but your flesh is not bulletproof.”

“Who said I was gonna get involved?” Kevin coyly asks back.

“Your stance is battle ready- You frequently forget that one is soul bound to your being and that one has full monitor over your physical and mental wellbeing." She scoffs again, stubbornly.

“And *you* frequently forget one thing about *me*, Scarlet; something you should have picked up on by now- when I wanna do something, Im'a do it. That's just how this train rolls!”

“This logic is foolhardy;” Scarlet scolds. “One shall have no part in assisting you here if you proceed with this engagement. You may use my blade, that is all one offers.”

“That’s completely fine with me, I've got kicks that can topple buildings. And besides, you said you’d help right my wrongs. So, if someone needs help, we’re gonna help 'em.”

"Do not twist my own words of encouragement!!”

“Sorry Scarlet, 'Suppose it's a habit from my era!”

Kevin appears from around the corner, though unnoticed by the six people before him. The lady with red hair tugs her jacket even tighter, still clutching the documents she stole... supposedly. Kevin walks forward, toe-pecking a crushed can, to awaken the crook's attention. Now, all parties are staring directly at him.

“Who are you? this is private business, Kid. Don’t get involved!” One of the unknown ladies speaks.

“Yeah.” Another woman adds. “You best get out 'a here. Don't want no bystanders getting involved in the boss's business.”

“Ooohh, a boss you say?” Kevin asks, all caution thrown to the wind. “So is this like a gang deal or-”

A man throws his trench coat down on the ground and whips a plastic baton from his belt, the woven material makes a loud *flump* sound as it hits the cold pavement. He points his weapon into Kevins chest and pushes him back.

“Won't ask twice, pal.” He grunts. “Now move before I break a rib!"

“Oho-ho, aggressive aren’t we, geezer? Is this how the five of you guys spend your free time, picking on people behind factories? Not supporting whatever it is you do, but there's way better places you could have picked."

The red-haired lady who clutches her jacket groans to herself and reveals the hand which was concealed by the ashen leather. She points a magically charged revolver at the man closest to Kevin and lets loose three shots of nature powered essence. No blood spilled, yet the man drops his weapon and falls to the ground like a ragdoll.

"If you're here then you might as well help instead of waffling on with yourself!" The red-haired woman shouts at Kevin.

"Oh- right!" Kevin shouts back as he dashes to her side with Scarlet in hand.

"Does monsieur le frimeur have a name?" The lady asks, snootily.

"No idea what *you* just called me- but people usually call me Kevin. What's yours?"

"It's Rose. I gather you fight?"

"Wouldn't be here if I didn't!"

Kevin boosts over to one of the violent women as Rose points her glowing barrels at another. Kevin's emblazed hand grips his enemies pistol, unleashing a powerful controlled explosion that blows the gun to bits.

As rose fires several rounds at the remaining enemies, Kevin slips around and hucks the already fallen fiend straight into another with heft- using his unconscious body as a weapon. The remaining flee unchivalrously without checking that their comrades are still breathing.

"LÂCHES! YOU'D BETTER RUN." The red-haired woman screams down the street, completely changing the lovely tone she spoke in moments before.

"Well, that was indeed something." Scarlet speaks, astounded.

Rose applauds. "En effet, c'était!" You've saved my bacon- merci, stranger. I didn't even have to- ...well whatever. Thanks for helping me out."

"You're welcome. To be fair I was kinda expecting there to be blood, can't lie."

"They're just members of some idiote little gang, that's all. Once one falls, they all go running. It's happened before."

"Do you know what gang they belonged too?"

"No, désolée. I couldn't tell you. Why did you decide to help little old me, anyway? I don't know you, do I?"

"Does it matter why? I saw someone in need, so I helped! A friend recently told me I should make up for my wrongdoings by doing something good, so that's what I chose to do."

"You're a strange one, Kevin. I think that friend of yours has a good head on their shoulders." Rose chuckles. "Brief, it's been super meeting you, but I should be getting back to close up shop."

"Alrighty then- stay safe!" Kevin waves goodbye as he walks away. But before he could leave, Rose grabs his shoulder and calls out to him again.

"Before you go. My shop- it's a small, corner flower shop just down the road from here- It's called 'Pétales de

Grette.' Maybe when you're not busy you could come by for some cakes and tea? My way of saying thanks."

Kevin's grin stretches across his face with giddy, childish excitement. "Oh, I can't say no to cakes, you've got yourself a deal, flower lady! I'll stop by whenever I've got time!"

"It's settled then, I hope to see you soon! Thanks again for saving me, au revoir!"

The two part ways. Rose pulls on her jacket and straightens her hat as Kevin bats himself off from the fight. As she walks away Kevin notices a large cursive embroidered pattern of the letter R, on her back; the centre piece of the image being a rose.

"Kevin-" Scarlet speaks, before being interrupted.

"I already know what you're gonna say-" He replies, still grinning at the promise of sweet treats. "Sorry for not listening before."

"...One should apologise also."

"What? You haven't even done anything."

"An apology is due from your battle with the Frost-Borne Hero... Do you recall my notion regarding the different power outputs this vessel is capable of? If you were to have struck Henry using my power during that battle, then he may not have left the arena with his life."

"Well, you said it before- we all make mistakes. I'm sure it wouldn't have hurt him too bad, right?"

"Kevin..."

“Let's focus on the now, pal. And ‘the now’ is going home and getting something to eat before Leah rips our heads off.”

“One lost her head centuries ago. My safety is guaranteed!”

“She could cut off your ribbons.”

"Oh, quite right, then. Let us be off, you have seven minutes before the hourglass empties.”

“I'll be there in three!”

Kevin presses the sole of his foot to the side of the old factory and kicks off the wall with an exciting and resounding blast-off soaring along the trainlines back to Carvina, upon arriving, he makes a boost past the Carvina College of Arcane with a salty feeling deep down...

He sprints through the autumn meadows making his way through the lanes of Lalstrun. And as his promise of a safe return was fulfilled, Leah still ended up clobbering him before even though he had to sit on the couch as Leah scolded him for his carelessness, sealing up his scrapes and bruises with care.

Since the exalted nimbus of Rah first showed itself above his head, all kinds of strange things have been happening to Kevin and his friends. He’s met some new strange ones, and some even stranger enemies: a hellish wolf, common thugs, a flying thunder snake and even a talking butterfly. With the vision of flowers, and even a cushy gathering in a whole other world on the horizon, Kevin eats a hearty meal with his family before making his way to bed as a new dream blooms on the golden sun set.

Glossary

A quick glossary on all the things that might go over your head whilst reading. Please refer to this portion of the book if you ever forget what something means or simply want to brush up on your Advance Heroes terminology. Characters are also listed here with tiny descriptions, as to not spoil the story.

A

Advance Heroes: An organisation harbouring several powerful warriors who fight for the peace of their town. The headquarters are in Rowanshire- however there are several more branches scattered around both worlds.

Aldea Esmeralda: A fictional city based in Spain where Thome went to study magic in his teenage years.

Aqua/Water magic: The element of magic which catalyses the power of water. Commonly practiced with a wand or staff.

B

Blanc: A fictional continent & country in Silvalon. Ruled by the King of Blanc alone.

C

Carvina: A fictional town based in England. Holds the Carvina College of Arcane.

Carvina College of Arcane: An educational facility which focuses on the academic practice of magic.

Christine Addamson | Grand Mistress of the Carvina College of Arcane | G.M.: The ever-smiling Grand Mistress of the Carvina College of Arcane. Loves Kevin and Thome like her own three children.

Conjure: A magically summoned creature borne of one's desires and aspirations.

D

Darchester: A fictional city based in England.

Destruction style magic: The category which any destructive and violent spells fall under.

Diana Jaqueline Allerton 'Jackie, Diane, DJ': One of Thome's friends who hails from the continent of Crimson in Silvalon. Has way more names than are listed here.

E

Earth magic: The element of magic that resonates with those who respect the earth and ground beneath them. Commonly practiced through catalysts, dance and rituals.

Enchantment style magic: Any spells that involve imbuing magic into an otherwise non-magical item is classed as enchantment style magic.

Ethos: Thome's loyal wisp-like conjure. A creature of many faces, talents and colours.

F

Fire/Flame magic: The element that channels a person's inner heat to create the gift of gods at their fingertips. No tools are needed to practice pyromancy, but wands and staves can be used... if you're like that.

Flogging Woods: Woods that sprawl around the hilly valley of Lalstrun. Home to many unexplainable things...

Force magic: The element of magic that channels the mind itself. Barely harmful on its own, but with the right tools and techniques, this element can prove very useful in all circumstances, and exclusive to humans only.

G

God-Speed: The given name of Kevin's Hyper-Real Power.

Grand Mistress | G.M.: The title of the head teacher and manager of an arcane college.

H

Henry Wolfarth | Frost-Borne Hero: The timid leader of the Advance Heroes.

Hyper-Real Power / HRP: A seemingly unnatural mutation that occurs in very few individuals- giving that lucky person a unique power of their own. Completely different from magic.

I

Ice magic: An unknown element.

Ivory Crown Peak: A mountain range in Blanc, Silvalon. Where the Pale Palace rests.

J

Jay: A young and kind fisherman whose favourite spot was taken that day.

K

Kevin Marrowald | 'Rah' 'Kev' 'Kevvy': The hero of the story. Leah's big brother and the creator of Mobbee.

L

Lalstrun: A fictional village based in England. Kevin and Leah live here. Contains a marketplace and holds Flogging Woods.

Lalstrun Farmers Market: The marketplace mentioned previously. Many farmers and sellers come here every week to sell their wares... if you have the coin.

Leah Marrowald | 'Lee' 'Loo-Loo': Kevin's younger sister. Practices enchantment and healing magic.

Lumen magic (Light & Dark magic): A balanced element. One cannot exist without the other. As such these two mysterious elements exist as one.

M

Manipulation class magic: Any magic that has the power to terraform or shift the shape of a person or thing is classed as manipulation magic.

Mercural: People made of liquid metal, similar looking to humans with a few but clear differences. Originating from Silvalon, these people are shrouded in mystery in today's times.

Metal magic: An element biologically exclusive to mercural kind.

Mobbee: Kevin's fluffy, adorable, conjured cat!

Mordale: A fictional town based in England.

Multiment: The given name of Thome's Hyper-Real Power.

N

Nature magic: An element practiced mostly in rituals and enchantments. Borrows the power of nature.

Nimbus: An astral projection that proves the status of a Spirit. Not much else is known about these things.

Note: Apparently, one of one-hundred collective conjures belonging to the King of Blanc.

P

Pale Palace: Where the King of Blanc watches from on high.

Pétales de Grette: The corner flower shop that Rose runs.

R

Reegie: A butterfly-like conjure? Creature? Nobody is truly sure.

Rose: A lady of France who runs a flower shop in Rowanshire.

Rowanshire: A fictional town based in England. Adorned with flowers and plants as far as the eye can see.

S

Scarlet | The Scarlet Blade: Kevin's new companion and weapon. Helpful in many unique ways.

Silvalon: The alternate plain home to mercurals.

Spirit: An unusual being who governs a specific worldly order.

Support style magic: A magic class containing healing spells and shields. Anything made to protect and serve a being's health.

Summoning style magic: Conjures and summoned items such as weapons or tools count towards this unique class.

T

'Thome' Samuel Ortiz | Multi Mage: The Multi Mage of the Carvina College of Arcane. Knows all 8 human Elements well.

Thunder/Electric magic: The element that channels thunder itself as a weapon. An emotion and body-based element.

Wind magic: A versatile and powerful element of magic that can be used in countless ways. Practiced with all available tools.

World Gate: The bridge between Earth and Silvalon.

Z

Zapp Susanna Bolt | Storm Commander: The Storm Commander of the Advance Heroes! Kevin's childhood idol.

Printed in Great Britain
by Amazon